"Paige, something's wrong."

Paige's stomach tightened. She slid lower in the SUV seat and tried to see out her side mirror. All she could make out was a pickup truck in the distance, coming closer by the second. Maverick the K-9 balanced on sure feet, watching Reece. He seemed to be in tune with his handler's change in mood.

"Someone's following us?" She grabbed the door as Reece increased speed entering one of the mountain curves. Tires squealed. Maverick barked.

Reece's SUV skidded toward the cliff...

Rocky Mountain K-9 Unit

These police officers fight for justice with the help of their brave canine partners.

Jodie Bailey writes novels about freedom and the heroes who fight for it. Her novel *Crossfire* won a 2015 RT Reviewers' Choice Best Book Award. She is convinced a camping trip to the beach with her family, a good cup of coffee and a great book can cure all ills. Jodie lives in North Carolina with her husband, her daughter and two dogs.

Visit the Author Profile page at LoveInspired.com for more titles.

DEFENDING FROM DANGER

JODIE BAILEY

LOVE INSPIRED SUSPENSE

INSPIRATIONAL ROMANCE

Special thanks and acknowledgment are given to Jodie Bailey for her contribution to the Rocky Mountain K-9 Unit miniseries.

LOVE INSPIRED® SUSPENSE
INSPIRATIONAL ROMANCE

Recycling programs for this product may not exist in your area.

ISBN-13: 978-1-335-58786-2

Defending from Danger

Copyright © 2022 by Harlequin Enterprises ULC

For questions and comments about the quality of this book, please contact us at CustomerService@Harlequin.com.

Love Inspired
22 Adelaide St. West, 41st Floor
Toronto, Ontario M5H 4E3, Canada
www.LoveInspired.com

Printed in U.S.A.

But as for me, my prayer is unto thee, O Lord, in an acceptable time: O God, in the multitude of thy mercy hear me, in the truth of thy salvation. Deliver me out of the mire, and let me not sink: let me be delivered from them that hate me, and out of the deep waters.
—*Psalm* 69:13-14

To Dutch and Daisy
Truly the "bestest puppies ever"
We miss you every single day

ONE

Nights like this made Paige Bristow shudder.

She paced to the window, her wolf-husky hybrid Luna close at her heels, and peeked between the slats on the blinds, looking down from the second-story living area to the animal refuge below. As a dry front swept through the narrow valley in the Lemhi Range, wind whipped the firs and pines into a frenzied dance, accompanying their sways with an eerie whine. The waning full moon layered the midnight hour in thin blue light.

Luna leaned heavily against Paige's leg, the pressure of her eighty-pound, gray-and-white body a sure indication the animal wasn't a fan of the vibe in the air.

On the other side of the gravel driveway, Howling Moon Wolf Refuge backed onto a sloped hillside that eventually led to the mountains on the edge of the Salmon-Challis National Forest. Tall fences ran up the slope. A dozen wolf-dog hybrids paced in their enclosures, where they were housed in pairs. Each was as restless as Luna.

One of them, probably Havoc, howled. The mournful cry raised the hairs on Paige's neck. When two others joined the chorus, she did shudder.

Usually, the occasional howl from her small pack of rescues thrilled her. Not tonight. Tonight, it all felt wrong.

Shaking off the chill, Paige dropped the slats and rested her hand on Luna's thick, furry neck. "Don't even think about singing along, girlfriend. If you wake the kid up, there won't be a bedtime treat for you."

Luna tilted her head and looked at Paige with eyes so light they were almost silver. She seemed to contemplate the words, almost as though she was gauging whether or not her owner would make good on the threat. With a sigh, she padded to the corner and sank onto her bed, licking her front paws, something she did only to calm herself.

"Good girl." In spite of the eerie night, Paige's favorite rescue never failed to draw a smile with her personality. Luna had been the first wolf hybrid Paige had personally brought to Howling Moon nearly six years earlier. They'd bonded immediately and, rather than board her with the rest of the pack, Paige had allowed Luna to become the family pet.

When Paige's daughter, Hailey, was born a few months after Luna's arrival, the wolf-dog had immediately taken on the role of protector. Even Paige's husband, Noah, had been "required" to ask permission before snuggling with Hailey.

Paige peeked out the window, the restless pacing of the animals making her edgy. Maybe the wind was the problem. The weather had kicked up like this ten months earlier, the day Noah had died in a flash flood on the Salmon River. The wolves had been restless then, too, before four of them had escaped through a hole in the back fence a few hundred yards upslope.

Surely they hadn't managed to bust through the fence, not after she had worked with her sole employee, Daniel, to reinforce it.

Havoc howled again. Most of the pack joined in.

Luna eyed Paige. *What do you plan to do about this racket?*

Pressing her lips together, Paige glanced at the stairs. Her daughter hadn't surrendered to slumber until half an hour earlier. While Paige wasn't a fan of leaving her five-year-old alone in the house, it wouldn't take her but a few minutes to run down the stairs and across the driveway to check on the animals.

She'd take the monitor.

Shrugging into her canvas jacket, Paige snapped her fingers for Luna to heel. A willful creature, Luna often obeyed only when she decided the plan of action was her own idea. The wolf side of her personality was stubborn.

Fortunately, Luna was curious about what the rest of the pack was up to on this wind-whipped August evening.

Paige grabbed the monitor, listened for her daughter's even breathing, then slipped out the back door with Luna trailing behind. It might be summer, but the temps at night typically hit the upper forties.

Clicking on her flashlight, Paige descended the deck stairs and followed the gravel path across the driveway to where the rescues were housed in spacious enclosures made for play and exploration. In the first pen, Havoc and Mercy roamed the fence line, but they didn't approach Paige.

Odd. The animals were smart. They knew she carried treats when she came out to check on them. Normally, they'd bound to the gate to greet her.

They advanced slowly when Paige called them. She slipped two small homemade treats through the tall fence then moved on to the next pen, where Tank and Cleo left off their pacing and approached the fence. Treats were more enticing than whatever they were watching.

The pair was her newest duo, brought in only three months prior from a rescue in Colorado. Tank, a male wolf-shepherd hybrid, was about eight. Cleo, a wolf-malamute, was likely nine. They'd become fast friends and had chosen each other over any other animal on the property.

She fed them treats, scrubbed their noses with one finger and then moved on. Between the anxiety in the animals and the strangeness of the weather, that haunted feeling wouldn't let up. Sweeping the light along the enclosures and toward the house, she didn't see anything out of the ordinary.

Still, everything felt wrong.

The blue darkness pressed closer as she neared the pen Camelot shared with his close companion, Hope. The two had been boarded together for years. Hope was an affectionate wolf-shepherd hybrid, with a gorgeous gray-and-tan coat, who never failed to meet a human at the gate, hungry for affection.

As Paige neared the enclosure, Hope did not appear. Neither did Camelot. Slowing her steps, she surveyed the huge pen that ran along the flat ground in the trees and up the side of the hill. It was impossible to see the entire area, but there was definitely no movement.

She swept the flashlight over boulders, past the covered shed where the animals bedded down, and toward the base of the hill.

There.

Hope stood protectively over a heap on the ground. When the light sparked off her eyes, she lifted her head and raised a soul-wrenching howl.

Paige's stomach bottomed out. "Camelot." Surely the two hadn't fought. She'd have heard it. There had been no indication…

It didn't matter. Paige unlatched the gate and jogged into the enclosure with Luna panting close at her heels. She slowed as she neared Hope and Camelot, not wanting to spook them or to get in the middle if an ongoing battle rage.

As she neared, Hope lay down beside Camelot and whimpered.

Whatever had happened, Hope hadn't caused it.

Paige dropped to her knees beside Camelot and lifted the flashlight. The wolf-malamute panted heavily and bared his teeth as Paige looked him over. He was in pain. She didn't dare touch him or move too quickly around him. Despite his usual gentleness, he could snap.

"It's okay, boy. I'll take care of you."

Behind her, Luna paced, growling low in her throat, but it seemed to be directed at the gate and not at either of the other animals in the pen. "Calm down, Luna." The last thing she needed was her beloved pet running off into the night. That was how Noah—

Now wasn't the time for memory.

Paige carefully inspected Camelot from the snout down. Blood matted the dark gray-and-red fur at the animal's rear flank, by his hip. It looked like… She leaned closer. Like pellet wounds. The type from a shotgun blast.

Bile soured her throat. How had she not heard the shot? She should have checked sooner, when she'd first sensed the pack's restlessness.

Why would someone do this?

This wasn't the first horrible injury she'd seen. She'd just released Storm back into his enclosure with Willow after he'd been slashed in the side by a wild animal.

Maybe it hadn't been a wild animal after all.

Another of her precious rescues was in pain, and this time there was no doubt it was at the hands of a human who'd sought them out. It wasn't like her hybrids freely roamed the area. Not one had escaped since the day Noah died.

Someone had come onto her property and purposely harmed Camelot.

Paige scanned the area, searching for movement, but the wind in the trees made the shadows come to life. Whoever shot Camelot could still be around.

But she couldn't move the animal to safety, and she wouldn't leave his side. She didn't dare risk a bite from the wounded animal. She needed help. Although she hated to rouse her friend and on-call veterinarian, Sebastian Farr, this close to midnight, there was no way she could nurse Camelot alone.

Luna rumbled low in her throat as Paige reached for her cell phone in her hip pocket. "It's okay, girl. We're going to take care of this."

Her cell phone wasn't there. Paige stared at the sky. In her hurry, she'd grabbed the monitor but not her phone. As much as she hated to leave Camelot alone, there was no choice.

She leaned as close to Camelot and Hope as she dared. "I'll be back." Hopefully they'd understand why she left to jog toward the wood-and-wire gate at the enclosure's entrance.

As Paige neared the gate, Luna jumped in

front of her. Her ears were laid back and she bared her teeth, growling deeply.

What? Paige slid to a halt.

A shadow moved to her left and Luna snarled louder. Something heavy slammed into Paige's left arm and shoved her down. Her head crashed into the thick wood post that held the gate. Stars exploded and pain whipped down her spine.

Paige slid to the ground with a cry as a weight punched her upper back and shoved her into the dirt.

Snarling, Luna leaped over her, charging at the threat.

There was a cry, definitely human. Luna yelped. Footsteps pounded into the distance. Then silence.

If someone had forewarned Rocky Mountain K-9 Unit officer Reece Campbell about how that last meeting would go, he'd have never believed them.

Or maybe he would have. There was already chaos swirling around the RMKU as it approached its one-year contract review with the FBI. The unit had been created to assist the FBI and law enforcement with cases across the vast Rocky Mountain region. But Daniella Vargas's resignation from the team was just one more in a long list that included a dangerous incident with a training weapon and an unlocked kennel that had allowed several K-9s, including his own partner Maverick, to escape.

If the unit was disbanded in November, would he return to Denver PD? Or would he move on to something else? The RMKU had offered new challenges. Going back to his old life felt a little empty.

He slid on his sunglasses as he exited the unit's HQ. Stopping in the center of the sidewalk, he stared at the brick building that housed the kennels where their K-9s rested or trained while the humans were at headquarters. The air conditioner hummed loudly in the midst of an August heat wave. At almost five in the afternoon, the atmosphere felt as though someone had set the temperature to broil. He was already hating the short walk.

Then again, the "short walk" gave him a minute to contemplate the latest earthquake to rattle the RMKU.

"Hard to believe, isn't it?" The voice over his shoulder so perfectly echoed Reece's thoughts that, for a second, he thought he'd spoken out loud.

But the voice belonged to fellow K-9 handler Harlow Zane. Her long blond hair was pulled up and away from her face. She was a couple of years older than Reece and the kind of beauty that tended to intimidate people. It also tended to make them underestimate the very capable officer.

"It's past hard to believe." Reece started walking again as Harlow fell in beside him. "If I was going to guess which of us would walk away from our jobs to start a family, Daniella would have been the last one I imagined."

His teammate chuckled. "Guess it's true love that changes people."

"Maybe." But so drastically? Daniella Vargas was a career cop who'd come to the RMKU from the Montana State Police K-9 Unit. She was tough and focused on the job almost to the point of obsession. But she'd fallen in love on a case, and that was that.

The announcement had rocked them all. Most of the unit was still sitting in the conference room, waiting for a punch line.

Reece knew there was no punch line. It was obvious in the way Daniella had talked about Sam Kavanaugh and his young son, Oliver. They'd changed her life. He recognized deeply rooted, forever love. Recently, he'd seen it in a couple of his teammates.

He'd also seen it in himself. Once. A long time ago.

He thought he'd seen it in the eyes of the woman he still tried to forget. The one who had crossed his mind too many times over the past couple of months.

The one who had turned out to be anything *but* in love with him.

His phone vibrated against his hip and he pulled it from his holster to glance at the screen. A 208 area code preceded the number. Nobody he knew. He shoved the phone back into place.

"Not taking calls today?" Harlow kicked a pebble. It skittered along the sidewalk and bounced off the metal door to the kennels.

"Don't recognize the number. It's a 208 area code, not from around here." He pulled the door open and stepped into the cool building. Sure, he didn't know the number, but he also didn't feel like talking. He was mulling over the sudden change in Daniella. It made no sense how someone so career-oriented could instantly flip to the family side of the coin.

"Did you say 208?" The slamming of the heavy door punctuated Harlow's question. "That's Idaho. Western side of the state. It's the same area code as Nelson's cell."

Fellow handler Nelson Rivers had come to the RMKU from Idaho State Police.

Wait. Idaho? *Western* Idaho?

Reece's heart tripped a few extra beats. He stopped walking. There was no way he'd received a phone call from western Idaho when he'd been thinking about...her.

"You okay?" Harlow faced Reece. "You look like you have a problem with Idaho." She planted her hands on her hips and raised one eyebrow in mock anger. "There's more there than potatoes, you know."

"It's not the state. It's—" He shook his head. That would be the wildest form of coincidence. "I knew somebody who lived there."

"Good rafting. Hiking too." Harlow shrugged and walked toward the kennel area. "Maybe your buddy looked you up."

"It's not—" *Never mind*. His past wasn't Harlow's business. Besides, she'd already disappeared through the double doors into the main kennel area anyway.

Reece leaned against the wall, the cinder block cool through his navy blue T-shirt. He slipped his phone from its holster. As he thumbed the screen to view the last number, the phone rang again, just in time for him to swipe to answer.

The incoming call was from the same 208 number.

"Hello?" A man's voice came thinly from the speaker. "Officer Campbell?"

Reece puffed air out slowly. It was a man. God might do some strange things, but it would be seriously weird if He'd had her call right when Reece had their past on his mind. *Very funny, God. Very funny.*

He raised the phone to his ear. "This is Officer Campbell."

"Officer Campbell, this is Sebastian Farr. I'm a veterinarian near Crystal Ridge, Idaho."

Reece's throat spasmed, choking on the words he'd planned to say. Crystal Ridge? This was way too close for comfort. *Not funny after all, Lord.* He tried to swallow, winced at the pain in his tight throat then tried again. "How can I help you?" The words emerged strained but with enough force to carry the weight of his authority.

"It's not me who needs help." The man exhaled loudly and said something away from the phone. "Hold on, please."

Reece pulled the phone from his ear and glanced at the screen. This call kept getting weirder.

"Reece?"

The feminine voice ran like ice water over the top of his head to the floor underneath him. It was her.

There was no way it could be. No way it should be.

But it was.

He said nothing. The sound of her voice after six years of silence was more than his mind could process.

"Reece? It's… Paige."

He sagged against the wall. "What do you want?" He'd meant to sound unmoved, emotionless, but the question clipped the air, marked by years of questions and heartache.

The phone was silent except for her breathing. Something like a chair creaked. In the background, a man spoke and a woman answered. Finally, Paige sniffed. "I know I promised—I mean…" The words trailed off into nothingness.

She'd destroyed him six years ago, had disappeared without a backward glance or even a goodbye. If she was calling him now, he didn't want to know why.

Except part of him did. That iota of morbid curiosity kept him from killing the call and blocking the number. "I'm at work, Paige." This time he managed to sound professional and detached. "What is it the Rocky Mountain K-9 Unit can do for you?"

"I don't know who else to call." Her voice seemed to have found itself. It was stronger, though a barely perceptible *something* threaded through the words, tweaking a heartstring or two. He'd heard that tone before; on those days when her past was causing her pain and she was desperately trying to pretend it wasn't.

Reece straightened and pressed the phone tighter to his ear. The room suddenly felt twice as cold. Paige Bristow might have taken dynamite to a future he'd been certain was carved in stone, but she wouldn't call him years later to rub it in. "What's wrong?"

"I don't know. Nobody here in Crystal Ridge believes me, but I'm pretty sure—" She paused as the man's voice spoke in the background. "Seb's pretty sure too, that…last night, someone tried to kill me."

TWO

"You did the right thing." Dr. Sebastian Farr slammed the door of his restored Chevy Blazer and met Paige at the front of the truck.

She stared at the enclosure where Camelot and Hope had been housed and ran her thumb along her fingertips. Hope paced the fence, watching Paige as though demanding an explanation for where her companion might be.

Not for the first time, Paige wished the animals could understand what she was saying. If so, she'd be able to explain to Hope that Camelot was receiving the best of care at the veterinary office. As soon as Seb left, she'd have to spend some quality time with Hope, who was confused and likely scared.

So was Paige. She balled her fists at her sides to keep from brushing her hand across the slight throbbing in the back of her head. Seb would want to take a second look and she was tired of the attention. It wasn't too painful, but it was a constant reminder of why Seb had insisted they call Reece.

Still, she wasn't certain she agreed. Seb was a great friend and an amazing veterinarian who typically refused to take a dime for what he did for her rescues, but Paige wasn't certain he was right about the wisdom of calling Reece. He'd pushed her for hours the day before, from the moment he'd returned in the wee hours of the morning after performing painstaking surgery to remove the pellets from Camelot's ripped flesh.

She never should have told him she knew Reece when they'd seen him on a national news clip about the Rocky Mountain K-9 Unit a few months earlier. The man's memory was a hundred miles long. Somehow, he'd managed to track Reece's number down and had shoved the phone into her hand yesterday before she'd even known what was happening.

Seb was trying to be a good friend, but he had no idea about the promise that had forced her to walk away from the man she'd planned to marry.

Neither did the man himself.

Contacting him had violated that promise, but there was no time to worry about it now. At the moment, the deed was done and the safety of her animals was paramount.

She'd ask Reece's advice, see if he could get the sheriff to actually investigate this time, then thank him for coming and send him on his way.

"Hey." Seb leaned against the front of the Blazer. "Camelot is going to be fine. I was able to get all of the shot out, and the shooter was far enough away to only inflict superficial damage. I'll keep an eye on him for a day or two for infection. He'll be back to tussling with Hope soon enough."

"I know." Seb had already reassured her more than once that Camelot was going to be fine.

Seeing one of her sweet animals in pain had wounded her in a way the bruise on the back of her head never could. "Thanks for letting Hailey stay with you guys for a few days."

"Lacey is over the moon." He elbowed Paige's biceps. "They'll camp out in the living room and have a great time."

Seb and Lacey had been trying for years to have children of their own, but they'd been disappointed time after time. After Noah died, Paige had asked them to be Hailey's guardians if the worst were to happen to her as well. They'd immediately agreed and spoiled the little girl as if she were their own. Most nights, Hailey's precious five-year-old prayers included one for her favorite two people to have a baby of their own, mostly because she wanted a playmate. Paige almost smiled.

Almost.

"Look." Seb shoved away from the truck. "Calling your ex isn't the most fun thing in the world but, based on what I saw online and what he told me on the phone, he's the guy we need right now."

"He's with a unit attached to the FBI. What's going on here at the refuge doesn't warrant intervention from—"

"I think it does, but I'll let him explain why when he gets here." Seb walked to the fence where Hope paced, her golden eyes never leaving them. "Bottom line, Lacey and I are worried about you and about the animals, and it can't hurt to let Officer Campbell and his team get involved."

Except it could. Because if word reached the wrong people that Paige had contacted Reece, then her daughter's future could be derailed before she even started kindergarten.

Behind her, tires crunched on gravel.

Paige's spine stiffened. This was it. She was about to lay eyes on the man she'd abruptly walked away from. The one she'd come within inches of promising her life to. The one she'd abandoned without an explanation.

The man who could never find out she harbored a secret that would change both of their lives.

She faced the long gravel drive that wound from the main road through the shelter of thick evergreens. A dark gray SUV with a badge on the door emerged from the trees and rolled to a stop next to Seb's Blazer. The words *K-9 Unit* were emblazoned on the back windows.

Through the windshield, Reece stared at her. Sunglasses hid his eyes, but there was no doubt where he was looking.

His expression was unreadable.

Paige hoped hers was equally impassive, but the wild storm spinning in her chest and stomach let her know she probably wasn't doing as good of a job as he was.

The past six years folded like an accordion. Time compressed until her head and heart both tried to convince her she'd last seen him only yesterday.

When he finally stepped out of the SUV, he left it running and strode toward her, scanning the property, letting his gaze pass over Seb... Looking at everything but her.

"I'm going to go inside and check on Luna. Make sure she's not turned over her water bowl." Seb walked toward the house, calling a quick hello to the officer who was striding toward them.

Way to have my back, friend.

She'd have words for Seb later. Better yet, she'd tell Lacey what he'd done and let her handle it.

For now, she had bigger issues only a few feet away and coming closer.

Not much about Reece had changed. He was still tall. Still built like the hockey player he'd been in college, broad-shouldered and lean. His eyes might have been hidden behind sunglasses, but they were vivid in her memory, a striking blue against his dark hair that always seemed to need a trim.

But his face… Never before had she seen that hard set to his jaw.

He didn't stop walking when he reached her. Instead, he passed by and stopped between her position and the wolf enclosures.

When Paige turned, he was studying the property, his hands planted on his hips. "Someone attacked your animals?"

She deserved this matter-of-fact cold shoulder. If only she could tell him she'd left to protect him.

She'd been strong for six long years since she'd walked away from him, terrified of his family and their threats, ostracized and alone.

She'd been strong for the past ten months, a widow with a young child and a floundering wildlife refuge.

For the past thirty-two hours, she'd been strong despite being physically bruised and emotionally exhausted. Somehow, the sight of the only man she'd trusted with her heart had managed to uncork the vial holding her strength and let it run out onto the ground.

"I told you on the phone." She tried not to choke on the words, but they stuttered nonetheless.

He pivoted on one heel and faced her, standing barely a dozen feet away, closer than he'd been the last time she'd seen him after a routine Friday night date.

Before his brother had knocked on her door. Before his mother had taken the wheel and driven their future off a cliff.

He stepped closer and studied her face. "Paige, I'll help. Talk to me."

Something in his words crumbled her resolve to keep him at arm's length. Instead of maintaining distance, she closed the gap between them, threw her arms around his neck, and cried.

Reece froze, hands still on his hips, breath stuck in his lungs. *What is going on here?*

He'd come because she was in trouble. He'd intended to do a quick survey, maybe let Maverick sniff around, then turn this over to local law enforcement or, if Dr. Farr was right about local law enforcement being hands-off, to the FBI. There was too much going on back in Denver for him to be away. The strange goings-on at the unit were one thing, but they were also in the midst of tracking a serial killer in the Rocky Mountains and searching for a missing infant who might have been the victim of a smuggling ring.

No, he couldn't be away. It was never his intention to—

Who was he kidding? Exhaling the regret he knew was coming his way, he slipped his arms around Paige's back and held her as she sobbed.

If he'd truly intended to stay uninvolved, he wouldn't have showed up in the first place. Wouldn't have found a loophole to let him. Wouldn't have driven all night to get here.

He'd spent twelve hours and countless cups

of gas station coffee telling himself he was only coming out of morbid curiosity about her life with Noah Bristow and their wolf hybrid refuge.

Where was Noah anyway?

Reece had plenty of other questions, but that one nagged him the most.

Well, that one and why she'd left him in the first place. He'd had plenty of time on the drive to wallow in that one. Plenty of time to remember his mother's hand-waving dismissal and his brother's smug smile, almost as though he'd expected it.

Quentin had been the other line of thinking that had plagued him on the drive. With nothing but late-night radio, he hadn't been able to bury the thoughts of his brother's crimes. The idea that there should have been a way to stop him. If Reece had opened his eyes sooner, the women Quentin had assaulted might be safe today.

He swallowed the disgust and guilt. None of that was why he was here.

"I'm sorry." Paige slipped from his arms and swiped at her cheeks beneath her sunglasses.

He felt colder, as though the brief thirty seconds he'd failed to comfort her had reawakened all of the times in the past when he'd held her.

It had felt…right. Like the way things should have been.

And very wrong. She was married to someone else.

She'd abandoned him. Walked away without any sort of explanation. Reece shouldn't care at all.

Yet somehow he did. His past love for her dictated his current desire to see her safe.

Clearing his throat, he tipped his head toward the house. "Where's your husband?"

Paige jerked. Her mouth dropped. She almost looked…stricken?

"Noah?" Paige walked to the gate where a lone wolf paced behind a high fence. She reached through the thick wire and scratched the animal's snout. "Noah died ten months ago."

Noah Bristow was dead? As angry and wounded as Reece had been the day he'd learned Paige had married Noah only weeks after she'd walked away from him, he'd have never wished this on her. "What happened?"

"Rafting accident." She addressed the hill.

"I'm sorry." There was really nothing else to say.

Paige shook her head. "Ever since he died, something weird has been going on. Up until last night, I had no proof it was targeted. But now?" When she faced him, it wasn't sadness marring her expression. It was anger and fear. "Now, I know this is personal."

So she didn't want to talk about Noah. Fine. He could appreciate grief. He'd felt it enough since she'd left. In fact, their past was a giant elephant that needed to be addressed if he was going to help her.

All of that could wait. Right now, he needed to know what sort of threat she was dealing with. "Start with what you do here and work your way up to what happened the night before last." Dr. Farr had called last night and filled him in on details Paige hadn't revealed, including the fact that someone had injured her.

Paige waved her hand at the wolf pacing behind her. "Noah started Howling Moon Refuge about ten years ago. It's a sanctuary for wolf-dog hybrids."

Nodding slowly, Reece leaned against the Blazer and scanned the area. Behind him, an older two-story log home stood, seeming to have sprung naturally from the landscape. There appeared to be a three-car garage on the ground floor with living area above. A large wooden deck ran along the side of the second story, a cracked concrete patio beneath. Behind the house, a metal barn nearly dwarfed the cabin.

In front of him, six pie-shaped enclosures dominated the property. Built into the natural curve of a large hill, they all had about fifty feet of flat land dotted with trees and boulders and shelters before the fences disappeared into the trees on the hillside.

He shoved his hands into his pockets and straightened, keeping his distance from her. "So you rescue these animals from where?"

"Around the country. We work with other sanctuaries and shelters. A lot of people don't understand hybrids aren't the same as dogs. They can be perfectly safe or they can be highly unpredictable. Some vets won't even treat them because their DNA can create issues." As she spoke, her posture relaxed. "Take rabies shots. There's never been one developed for wolves, so it can be ineffective in hybrids. There's a long list of potential issues for owners, like not properly housing or caring for an animal that is, for all intents and purposes, half wild. Many are euthanized or set loose to run wild, where they don't fit in either." She laced her fingers through the fence behind her. "We try to help where we can by offering a place where they can live out both sides of themselves, as free as we can make it and as close to humans as they want to be."

Her expression warmed. It was clear her passion was here.

She'd always had a soft spot for animals and had wanted to be a veterinarian. Her past in the foster care system had given her a compassion for the lost and unwanted. He hadn't missed her words about these animals having no place to belong. This place was perfect for her. It was as though someone had laid her heart along these foothills.

Glancing at his vehicle where Maverick lounged in his protected kennel, Reece walked closer to an enclosure, several feet from Paige. They'd both loved animals. It had been one of the things that had forged their relationship.

Clearly, somehow, he'd missed the bond it had also forged with Noah Bristow.

He dug his teeth into his lower lip to stem the personal comments. This needed to remain professional.

As he neared the enclosure, two hybrids trotted up and nosed at the fencing. They seemed friendly enough.

Paige didn't leave her spot. "Braveheart and Aspen. They've been together for about five years. You can pet them. They both love people."

Easing closer, Reece laid the back of his

hand against the fence, letting the animals scent him. The larger gray one licked his fingers and nudged his nose through the fencing. "Together?"

"We house them with a companion, since wolves are naturally social. Letting them all run together as a giant pack could be problematic, and research has showed they thrive in twos or threes. It's a process. Some pairs work. Some don't."

There was no way he was going to read too much into *that* statement. "Tell me what's been happening."

With a sigh, Paige walked over to pet the wolf-dog who was housed alone. "Nothing I could really call intentionally malicious, until now." She winced. "The day Noah died, several of the animals escaped through a hole in the fence. A few weeks later, Storm got caught up in some barbed wire up at the top of the enclosure. We don't use barbed wire on the property. Willow's paws were cut up on some glass not long after. Small but mean things. If they only happened once, it might be considered accidental. But last night…"

Last night, she'd witnessed the brutality first-hand.

She rose and opened the gate, waving for him to follow. "I'll show you." Entering the enclosure, she knelt and called the dog inside closer, burying her hands in the thick fur at the animal's neck. She glanced up at Reece as he closed the gate behind him. "This is Hope. She's Camelot's companion and was standing guard over him last night. Give her a second to get your scent, and she'll love you forever."

As Reece approached, Hope eyed him curiously. No malice, just quiet curiosity.

"Get on her level." Paige's voice was low. "Hope was picked up outside of Eglin Air Force Base in Florida. Someone thought she was all wolf and called animal control. We think she was abused, because she's a little skittish when a man towers over her."

Reece could appreciate that. He approached slowly, took the treat Paige passed to him, and crouched beside the animal. He held his hand out so Hope could sniff his knuckles.

She nudged open his fingers and took the treat, then sniffed his pants' pockets before she leaned against him and nearly bowled him over with her weight.

Paige chuckled. "I should have warned you she's a leaner." She stood and wiped the dust from the knees of her jeans while Reece rubbed the top of the dog's head. "If she leans, she likes you. She recognizes a dog person."

"Or she smells Maverick on my clothes."

"Possibly. It might help her take to him a little easier if we introduce them. She'll associate your dog with you." Holding out a hand, she helped him up, letting go when he was on his feet. "Back here."

He was going to ignore the way the warmth of her touch lingered against his palm, the same way her earlier embrace still clung to his back. "So someone shot Hope's...*companion*?"

"Camelot." Paige stopped not far from the covered shed where the animals likely bedded down. "Here's where I found them."

The ground was scuffed and spotted with blood. Stepping wide around the spot, Reece paced a string of smears until he got to the wooded area, where pine needles masked the trail. "Is it okay if I bring Maverick out? He's a sniffer, trained at locating blood and following blood trails."

"I'll take Hope to the big barn and let her play in there. She likes to run and slide on the polished concrete." Paige's voice held amusement as she led the animal away.

Reece watched until she disappeared into the large building. He shouldn't have come, yet he couldn't stay away. She needed him, even though she hadn't been anywhere to be seen when he'd needed her the most.

Shaking off frustration and anger, he pressed the remote to open the SUV's door and called for Maverick. They had work to do.

In seconds, Maverick was at his side, quivering with excitement. The sleek German shepherd loved his job above all else…mostly because there were treats at the end.

Reece gave Maverick free rein to follow the blood trail. The dog took off toward the hillside, nose down and twitching. A fresh trail made easy work. Reece hiked up the hill through the trees with the dog, following a narrow path the hybrids had made, the climb growing steeper as they went. The enclosure was deeper than he'd expected, but the space likely made Paige's rescues feel like they had room to roam.

At the tall fence, Maverick pawed the ground. He could go no further.

Reece commanded him to sit, gave his partner a treat and a vigorous head rub, then squatted to investigate the spot.

This was clearly where Camelot had been shot. Blood spatter told the awful tale.

On the other side of the fence, a hunk of raw meat was surrounded by scratch marks where Camelot had tried to paw his way to it.

Reece balled his fists. Someone had laid a trap, knowing the animals would be drawn to the bait and would stay in one place long enough to retrieve it, thus making a steady target.

Why not simply poison the meat? Why deliver a nonlethal blow to the hip from a distance instead of firing a close-range kill shot to the chest?

It made no sense that they'd attacked Paige directly yet fired on Camelot from the cover of darkness and trees.

Reece sat back on his heels and studied the rocky hillside. *Why?* Because this wasn't about killing the wolves. This was about sending a message. Somebody wanted something from Paige and was escalating the threat. If she didn't soon give them what they were asking, they might take it at any cost.

THREE

"I'm telling you, the sheriff isn't going to do anything." Paige climbed out of Reece's SUV and shut the door gently. It would be nice to take out all of her frustration with a satisfying *slam*, but the last thing she wanted to do was frighten Reece's K-9.

Through the window, she could see Maverick curled up in his dedicated kennel where the back seat would normally be. "You're sure he's okay in there?"

Reece rounded the truck and stood near the front bumper. "It's his home. The engine runs even when the keys are out, so the vehicle stays cool. He has water and his bed. He's happy as can be."

"What if the engine shuts off?" The day was blazing hot at high noon. If the AC conked, Maverick would land in life-threatening trouble quickly. She couldn't bear the thought.

Reece's smile was wistful. He knew her soft spot for pups. "If the temperature goes up in the vehicle, the lights and sirens go off. The windows roll down. An alarm on my remote activates, and text messages fire off to me and half my team. Trust me, my partner has more safety precautions working in his favor than I do."

Well, if Reece was sure, she'd have to trust him. She sent the dog a wave then joined Reece at the front of his SUV.

They walked across the parking lot toward the log office building. The hulking brick county jail sat behind it to the left, a stark contrast to the more rustic design of the administrative section. Reece studied the structure. "Why are you so convinced the sheriff won't help?"

"Because he hasn't so far." Paige had pled with the man. Seb had gotten into heated conversations with him. Paige's sole employee, Daniel O'Reilly, had written emails and made phone calls. Nothing had worked. The sheriff, along with over half of the town, carried a highly unfavorable opinion of Howling Moon.

"Paige?" Reece's voice came from behind her. He'd stopped as they'd reached the sidewalk, and she'd outpaced him. When she turned, he lifted his eyebrows and held his hands out to his sides. "I'm not walking in there if you have intel I need to know. Am I about to botch someone else's investigation? Make a fool of myself and my team fighting a fight where there's no battle?"

"What?" Paige glared at the man who had once been her staunchest defender. *No battle?* He was joking, right? Someone had shot Camelot. Assaulted her.

She stalked to him and stood only inches away, going toe to toe with the only person who could help.

"Sheriff Granger has repeatedly told me I'm a widow who is letting her grief make her paranoid. He's either refused to investigate or has come up with easy answers when he has." Her ire cooled and she slid her hands through her hair, trying to think of the words she wanted to say; the hardest ones of all. "When Noah founded the refuge, some people were antsy. There's a lot of misconception about wolf-dog hybrids. Like any canine, in the right circumstances, they can be dangerous. Noah got a lot of pushback. Since he died, it's gotten worse. I'm viewed as weaker than him, unable to care for or control my rescues."

She fought to keep the tears at bay. It wasn't so much about Noah, whom she truly missed, but about the prejudice against those beautiful animals he'd died trying to save. The ones she'd dedicated her life to. "Most people don't believe I'm capable of running the refuge by myself. Even my assistant, Daniel, has doubts. He doesn't voice them, but I can see them."

Reece studied her face as though trying to read her honesty. Finally, the tightness in his posture eased and he stepped around her. "Let's go talk to this Granger guy. I'll flex a little bit of federal muscle, try to change his tune."

There it was again, the allusion he might have something in his hip pocket to use for leverage. Something he had yet to tell her. She wanted to ask, but he'd strode ahead and was almost to the front door of the sheriff's department.

They stepped into a tall, open, airy lobby more like a backcountry ranger station than a county law enforcement building. Paige's sunglasses darkened the room, but there was no way she was going to slip them off and show the world her red-rimmed eyes.

With all of the authority of the badge around his neck, Reece took control of the room. He marched to the first open reception window and spoke with the deputy seated behind the bulletproof glass.

Still, even Reece's swagger likely wouldn't get them an audience with the great and powerful Hank Granger.

The deputy tilted his head to listen to Reece then glanced at Paige where she stood near the door. There was a slight furrow in his brow. He reached for the phone and said a few words, his eyes never leaving hers.

Yep, this was going to go the way it always did. They'd never—

The deputy replaced the receiver and waved her over.

Paige felt her eyes widen as she joined Reece at the counter. Exactly what kind of authority was in those muscles he'd *flexed*?

The deputy spared her one more glance before he pointed at a door on the far side of the room. "Sheriff Granger is out back having lunch under the awning. He says you can have ten minutes. That's all the time he has left on his lunch hour."

"Lunch hour?" Reece's voice was laced with sarcasm as he pushed away from the counter. "Must be nice." The words were muttered too low for the deputy to hear, but they were loud and clear to Paige. He tossed a thank-you to the deputy then headed out the door the man had indicated.

They walked into the shade of a covered porch along the side of the building, boasting a view of the side and back of the property. Stables housing the horses and equipment for the off-road rescue team was to the right. A shooting range sat behind a high fence at the back of the building. Beyond it, the valley rolled to the Bitterroot Mountains, which overpowered the horizon.

Too bad she couldn't enjoy the sight.

As they approached, Sheriff Hank Granger eyed them from his seat at a concrete picnic table he shared with Brody Carson, who ran several successful tourist-oriented businesses around Crystal Ridge.

Great. If only she could warn Reece. Brody was the voice of the *shut down Howling Moon* faction in town. He was also Sheriff Granger's son-in-law. If they were together, this was going to go even worse than she'd anticipated.

Sure enough, Brody eyed her with a smirk before he sized up Reece. "Who's your friend, Paige?"

The sheriff shot him a hard look before he turned to Reece. "Hank Granger. This is my son-in-law, Brody Carson."

Reece stepped up to the table as though he belonged there. Point in his favor. He extended his hand to the sheriff, who shook it briefly. "Reece Campbell, Rocky Mountain K-9 Unit, a mobile team under contract to the FBI. I'm here to determine if the issues at Howling Moon Refuge warrant federal intervention."

Brody's eyebrows rose so high, they nearly met his close-cropped blond hair.

Sheriff Granger coughed and settled his water bottle on the table. Wiping his mouth with the back of his hand, he seemed to weigh Reece's words. "FBI? My deputy said you were with a K-9 unit, but he didn't mention federal authorities." He tightened his lips then apparently decided he should make friends. Pointing to the bench across the table, he addressed Reece. "Have a seat."

"I'll stand. Thanks."

The authority in Reece's voice caused the sheriff to jerk his head back before he reset his expression.

Brody simply watched. Taking a handful of potato chips from a bag, he ate them one by one, watching Paige the entire time.

She turned to the sheriff. "Someone shot Camelot last night."

"One of your wolves?" The sheriff bit a hunk out of his sandwich, chewed and swallowed. "You keep coming to me with these alleged attacks on your wolves, but they all seem pretty easy to chalk up to carelessness. Did this Camelot get out again and wander onto some-one else's land?"

"Get out again?" Paige's voice pitched higher. "They got out once and—"

Reece's hand on the small of her back silenced her. He pulled in a deep breath as though he wanted her to do the same. It was a quiet *It's okay,* the same kind he'd given her more than once when his mother had started a tirade against her.

Too bad he hadn't been there the last time.

Paige let off the gas. This was Reece's wheel-house, not hers. The sheriff and Brody both seemed to respect his presence.

Easing one foot slightly forward, he rested his hands on his belt. "Mrs. Bristow's rescues have been attacked multiple times. Night before last, one was shot on her property."

He didn't mention someone had assaulted her, but Paige kept quiet. Reece had his reasons.

The sheriff stood. "Did you call my department when it happened? Ask anyone to come out and investigate?"

"No. She called my team. According to her, you haven't been too eager to catch whoever is harassing her and her rescues." Reece widened his stance slightly, commanding the situation.

"Look, my department is currently dealing with a murder on the outskirts of Crystal Ridge and several assaults on campers on county land. Someone possibly teasing some animals is low on my list of priorities. If Mrs. Bristow is concerned, she needs to file a report."

"Sounds like you could use some outside help." Reece didn't sound helpful. He sounded determined. "My team will be taking over Mrs. Bristow's calls from this point forward."

Granger cursed under his breath. "By what authority?" The sheriff stood and widened his own stance. At just over six feet, he was a hair taller than Reece.

"Camelot, the hybrid who was shot on Paige's property, has red wolf blood. Under the Endangered Species Act of 1973, red wolves are an endangered species in North America and have been granted protected status. That makes the shooting a federal crime, which makes it my team's jurisdiction."

It did? Paige schooled her face to remain set in defiance and not sag in shock. She'd allowed Seb to call Reece out of desperation to take a quick look around. She hadn't expected him to…to *stay.*

"I'll be in touch." Reece turned and ushered Paige toward the door.

Paige waked mechanically, not looking him in the eye as he held the door open and she entered the coolness of the air conditioning.

Reece was staying? This was not what she needed. Not at all. Because every day he was in Crystal Ridge was one more day for his mother to find out Paige had broken her promise.

One more chance for him to discover Hailey was his daughter.

Reece nearly slammed the door of the SUV, but that might throw Maverick off his footing. Plus, his partner tended to pick up on his frustration and to get vocal about it. Now wasn't the time for Mav to bark his commiseration.

Reece exhaled slowly as Paige buckled her seat belt. Had he really committed to staying on and solving this case? His chief, Tyson Wilkes, had been clear Camelot's status as a red wolf hybrid created a gray area for them to enter through, but Reece had never intended to throw the door wide open and take up residence.

He couldn't call anyone else on the team to take his place either. Not only were they dealing with other cases across the Rockies, they were also searching for a missing baby, hunting a serial killer, and wrestling with what appeared to be a direct threat against the Rocky Mountain K-9 Unit itself.

No, he was the only one between major cases at the moment. If the K-9 unit was going to help Paige, then the responsibility fell to him.

A quick yip from Maverick pulled Reece's attention into the present. Pivoting in his seat, he stuck his finger through a hole in the barrier between Mav's kennel and the driver's area and rubbed the dogs snout. "Sorry, boy. Did I forget to greet you?" He pulled a treat from the leg pocket of his cargos and fed it to the dog. "Good job keeping the truck safe, buddy."

"He gets a lot of treats." Paige watched with something between interest and wariness. There was a shadow in her expression, probably from the encounter with the sheriff and his mini-me.

"He's a working dog. The more he works, the happier he is. He was guarding the vehicle, or so he thinks. Therefore, he gets a treat."

Paige nodded slowly then focused on her fingers, which she'd laced together in her lap. "Is it true? About the attack on Camelot being a federal crime?"

Pulling his head to the side, Reece stretched tense neck muscles as he started the vehicle. "Sort of."

When he glanced at her, she was staring at him with one eyebrow arched. *"Sort of?"*

"It's true red wolves are endangered and have protected status." However, the Endangered Species Act said nothing about hybrids.

Paige kept watching, almost as though she knew what he was thinking.

Fact was, she probably did. He'd rarely been able to fool her. Birthday presents, surprise parties… She'd figured them out, every one.

Maybe six years ago she'd also figured out his big plans for their date the night she'd disappeared. He turned away from her and watched the rearview as he backed out of the parking space to head back to Howling Moon. The fact he'd had both a ring and a question at the ready could have been the reason she'd fled.

Once they were on the road through the eclectic downtown that made Crystal Ridge a tourist haven, he cleared his throat and set aside the past. Again. They'd talk about it eventually, but only when he was ready. "Brody is married to the sheriff's daughter? You already know what I'm thinking."

"He has his father-in-law's ear? Maybe has sway with what the sheriff investigates?" Paige stared out the window, watching Main Street glide by as they cruised at the low speed limit.

"Maybe. Sheriff Granger isn't a bad man. Maybe a little selective in how he does his job, but seemingly a good man otherwise."

"A law enforcement officer who doesn't do his best to protect everyone under his care is not *a good man*, Paige." That burned him the most about Granger. Law enforcement officers didn't get to pick and choose who they protected. They protected all. Equally. Whether or not you liked them personally or agreed with what they were doing in their lives.

That wasn't a debate for right now. He glided to a stop and motioned to a family waiting at a crosswalk. Buildings of all shapes, sizes and materials lined both sides of the generically named street, which stretched away from them for over a mile. It was a blend of Old West prospecting, late nineteenth-century building boom, and mid twentieth-century revitalization. Art studios, local restaurants and outdoor suppliers all blended to create a unique tourist town.

Several of the buildings bore the Carson name, from restaurants to sporting goods stores and even a white-water-rafting adventure center. "Brody Carson has a foothold in this town."

"His family probably owns half of it. They've gotten rich off of the tourist industry." Paige leaned forward to look at one of the mountain peaks that Main Street led straight toward. "It's one of the reasons he's so dead-set against Howling Moon. He's convinced we're too close to 'civilization,' even though the refuge is seven miles from here. He's got half the town believing if my rescues ever escaped, they'd run like rabid monsters down Main Street, maiming and killing the young and the weak."

Reece winced as he eased onto the gas again. He'd heard some of the same arguments about law enforcement K-9s. *Menace. Dangerous. Uncontrollable.*

"Brody's leading the charge with a petition to the county. He wants to shut down Howling Moon and force us out. I've talked to a lawyer who's passionate about protecting nonprofits, but legal counsel costs money. In fact, it would take more than I have in savings. Between operating expenses and trying to keep food on the table for—" She tensed then redirected her train of thought. "At any rate, we're running on half of a shoestring at this point. If Brody and his crew push much harder, they'll get what they want because I won't have the funds to stay open. The local backers the refuge once had have pulled out. I've applied for some grants, but no luck so far. There's one more I'm waiting to hear back on. One that would keep us open for another year. I should know any day now."

"Have you thought about moving the refuge?"

"I've looked into it, but the land we're on is free and clear. It belonged to Noah's family. A move would require me to sell, which would make Austin Wyatt happy. He owns the Flying W Ranch next door. He'd pay me fairly, but even if he paid me top dollar, I couldn't afford to relocate and rebuild anywhere else." She stared at a fir tree mural painted on the brick façade of Pine Top Creamery. "It doesn't matter. I haven't been able to find a place nearby with the perfect blend of open land and slope and trees for the animals."

Interesting. The rancher next door wanted her land too? *How many more people in Crystal Ridge had a vested interest in seeing Howling Moon shut down?* "Has Brody ever threatened you?"

"No. He's arrogant and entitled, but he's never been violent." She pointed to a small café on the next corner, and her tone changed. "I didn't get breakfast this morning and it's past lunch already. Would you mind if we stopped at Minnie's? They have amazing sandwiches and potato salad you'll want to swim in."

Clearly, she was done talking about her problems for the moment. "I'm one hundred percent with you on food, especially if it's that potent." However he was *not* with her on her assessment of either the sheriff or his son-in-law.

As a military policeman, a patrol officer and now a K-9 officer, he'd seen the worst of humanity. Had seen the guy who sang in the choir or the woman who taught kindergarten do heinous things. Everyone had three personas, from the one they showed in public, to the one they shared with the people they trusted, to the deeply buried one only they knew about.

Something told him one of the men in Paige's army of haters had a seriously twisted buried persona.

As he hooked a right to park in front of Minnie's, Paige's phone rang. She glanced at the screen. "It's Daniel."

She'd mentioned Daniel O'Reilly several times. From what Reece could gather, he helped with the animals and with the upkeep on the refuge.

Was there more to their relationship? It could go to motive. There was no other reason he needed to know.

"Daniel." Paige reached for her seat belt as Reece pulled the car to a stop in a parallel spot near the café, but she stopped in midmotion. "What's wrong?"

The fear in her voice froze his hand on the gearshift.

"Daniel, listen to me. Call Seb and call 9-1-1. We're on the way." She killed the call, her hand shaking and her face drained of color.

Reece reached for her but let his hand drop to the console between them.

"We have to go back to the refuge." Her voice trembled and she shoved her hair from her forehead. "Someone attacked Daniel. He's hurt."

FOUR

No emergency vehicles waited at Howling Moon, despite Paige's instructions to her employee.

Reece frowned as he slowed the SUV and rolled onto the gravel between the house and the enclosures. He'd clearly heard her tell Daniel O'Reilly to call for help. Why hadn't he done so?

His back muscles tensed as he scanned the area. If Daniel had been injured, the assailant could have done more harm after the call to Paige.

Behind him, almost as though he could read Reece's thoughts, Maverick shifted and stood, planting his feet against the gentle sway as the SUV rolled to a stop near the house's elevated deck.

Paige reached for the door before he could shift the vehicle into Park.

Reece was quicker. He grabbed her hand before she could unfasten the seat belt. "No."

"What do you mean *no*?" Paige jerked from his grasp and went for her seat belt again, but Reece laid his hand over the release to block her escape. She gripped his hand and tried to pry his fingers away. "Daniel's hurt. This is my fault. I have to—"

He maintained his hold. "You have to wait here. No discussion. Until I can assess the situation and make sure whoever assaulted your worker isn't still on the property, you're safer in the vehicle with the doors locked and with Maverick to watch over you." He forced every ounce of the command tone he'd learned in the line of duty into his voice. She had to listen to him. Had to understand this might be her home, but danger lurked in the early afternoon shadows.

Paige stopped digging at his hand, but her fingers remained tightly locked around his, and her eyes maintained a hold on his in a defiant, silent argument.

The air between them was thick with mutual stubbornness. It was also heavy with every word unspoken and every question unasked for six years.

Hours could have passed. He was locked on

deep green eyes that hardened into ice when she was determined.

Some serious arctic wilderness glared back.

Maverick yipped and butted the metal door with his nose.

With a sharp tug, Paige pulled her hand from Reece's and crossed her arms at her chest, facing the front window. "Fine."

"Fine." Echoing her, Reece turned and unlatched the door between the rear and the passenger area, letting Maverick slip between the front seats. If she wanted to act like they were locked in a third-grade playground battle, so be it. He pointed at Paige and looked Maverick in the eye. "Guard."

It was almost like Maverick nodded before he sat in the narrow space between the seats and turned his fiercest work face toward Paige.

She looked down her nose at the K-9. "Is he going to bite me if I try to get out of the car?"

"No." Reece shoved open his door, stepped out and then turned to look back at her. "Although he'll probably tear a hole in the hem of your shirt if you reach for the handle."

She sank into the seat, her slumped posture the outward expression of her defeat. When she finally looked Reece in the eye, all defiance had vanished. In its place, worry lines etched her forehead. "Make sure Daniel is okay, and find whoever hurt him."

Nodding, Reece shut the door and pulled his weapon from the holster at his hip. Holding it low, he scanned the area then slipped around the elevated deck, watching and waiting for motion.

Nothing unusual seemed to be happening on the property. Even the animals in their enclosures were going about their business, lounging in the sun or tussling together at play. They didn't seem concerned and showed only mild interest at Reece's presence, probably because Paige had introduced him to all of the rescues before they'd left for the sheriff's office.

"Over here." The voice was thin and it came from above. "Don't shoot. I'm not armed."

On the wooden deck about twelve feet off the ground, a young man in his midtwenties sat on a weathered Adirondack chair, his hand pressed to the back of his head over close-cropped dark hair. He eyed Reece warily. "I really hope you're Paige's friend."

"I really hope you're Daniel O'Reilly." He waved Paige over as well, then held his badge up where Daniel could see it more clearly. "Officer Reece Campbell, RMKU."

This guy was younger than Reece had assumed he'd be, despite what Paige had told him earlier. When Daniel nodded, Reece holstered his SIG and climbed the steps. He pressed the button on his remote to open the SUV doors, releasing the K-9 from guard duty.

Maverick reached him first, sitting as soon as he made Reece's side. Reece was leashing his partner when Paige thundered up the stairs and squeezed past him.

She dropped to her knees beside Daniel in full mother hen mode. "What happened?"

"I was unlocking the shed where we keep the mower because I was going to take care of the big field behind the house. Something hit me in the back of the head. Hard. Knocked me right to my knees." He brushed dirt off his pants with the hand not pressed to his head, wincing with the movement. "I heard somebody running off, caught a glimpse of a guy in jeans and a gray T-shirt, but he disappeared around the house."

Reece headed down the steps while Paige continued to talk to Daniel, and Maverick followed at his heels. He walked around the house, eyes down, looking for footprints or flattened grass, but the search was futile. The gravel was packed down in the front part of the house, hard as concrete. The grass around the back had been cut close recently, so there was no way a footprint would show.

For a long moment, he stared into the woods. Close to the house, the undergrowth had been cleared, meaning there was no hope of finding a trail. If Maverick were a tracker, he'd try to find a scent, but since he was trained in protection and blood detection, giving the K-9 his nose wouldn't help.

"See anything?" Paige rounded the house and came over to stand beside him. "I asked Daniel if he could describe the guy, but he said all he saw was clothes."

"Makes sense if he was picking himself up off of the ground after getting his bell rung." Reece rested a hand on Mav's head where the dog heeled beside him. "I don't see anything. What's on the other side of those trees?"

"There's an old logging road, more trees, and then the Flying W Ranch's land. This used to be a logging camp. When Noah bought it, only the main building and the sheds were still here. He converted the space into a house and had the big barn and enclosures built."

"A logging road?" He didn't want to talk about Noah yet. It only brought questions about why Paige had run from him to marry someone she'd only mentioned to him a few times. From his recollection, Noah had been a childhood friend and nothing more. She'd never hinted at having feelings for him.

Reece headed for the three sheds behind the house to the left of the barn. "Which shed was Daniel near?"

"The middle one."

"How bad is he hurt?" His stride was heavy, his heels thudding hard on the packed ground as he tried to pound his frustration and anger into the earth. Paige had enough on her plate without him dragging their past into the mix.

"There's a decent cut on the back of his head but nothing too dangerous. Why didn't he call 9-1-1 like you told him to?" This could be so much worse than it appeared from the surface. The guy could have a concussion.

"He said he knew we were coming and he'd also called Seb. Seb is here and is going to take Daniel to the ER to get looked at. Daniel is big on protecting the animals, and he said there'd been enough activity out here today already. He was afraid an emergency call would bring fire trucks and an ambulance and deputies." Paige sighed and stopped walking, turning to look at the creatures she cared for. "Some days I wish Noah had built the enclosures farther up the hill, with more distance between them and the house instead of right there on the other side of the yard."

"Why?" He glanced in the direction she was looking but kept walking. If there was evidence to be found, it would be at the shed where Daniel was hit.

"They'd be less disturbed by people, but then I wouldn't be able to see them from the house and there's… Well, it's comforting." She jogged up beside him then matched his pace.

As they neared the shed, he held his hand out to stop her. "Wait here. We don't need to taint evidence." While she hung back, he unhooked Maverick's leash. Daniel's assailant might have dropped whatever he'd used to strike. If blood had been drawn like Paige said, Mav would find it. The K-9 could sense droplets smaller than the eye could see. "Search."

Maverick's nose went to ground, and he started sniffing, his tail wagging and his body practically wiggling with the excitement of the hunt.

Almost immediately, he barked twice then sat beside a board lying inside the shed door. With his cell, Reece snapped a photo of the board and its location, then donned gloves and picked it up. It took a second to find blood, but there were dark traces on the side of the wood.

In the nearest enclosure, one of the wolves, a gray-and-white monster of a creature, howled, drawing Maverick's attention.

"Search." Reece brought his partner back to task, hoping to find more evidence.

Maverick trotted over and heeled after sniffing the shed inside and out.

Nothing. Not even where the board had been.

He scratched Maverick behind the ear and clipped on his leash. He then fed him a treat. He'd found the board, but Paige's wolf hybrids seemed to distract his partner, which was unusual for a dog trained as well as Mav.

Maybe Daniel's wound hadn't been deep enough to draw a lot of blood. Either way, the younger man had obviously been shaken up.

"Find anything?" Paige stood where he'd left her. Her expression, drawn and tense, was also expectant. Likely, she was hoping they'd found conclusive evidence written in the marks on the ground about who was behind this.

As he walked over to join her, he studied the tree line. It would be nice to find answers clearly written in the dirt.

Instead of answers, he had more questions. Instead of one suspect, he had nearly half a dozen.

And instead of driving back to Denver tonight, he was staying in Idaho with the woman who was a bigger danger to his heart than he wanted to acknowledge.

"It's high tourist season, but I managed to get you reservations at one of the bed-and-breakfasts in town." Paige slipped through the screen door and walked across the deck. It might have been ungracious to leave him outside in the heat, but letting him into her house felt wrong somehow.

Not wrong. Terrifying. As though he would see inside to uncover every secret she'd hidden there. Given that photos of Hailey and samples of her preschool artwork were everywhere, her biggest secret was on full display. It was definitely better for him to remain firmly on the outside.

She handed a glass of ice water to Reece and settled a bowl of water in front of Maverick, who lay at his feet. Her head throbbed slightly as she leaned over, so she straightened quickly. "I hope you have a really generous per diem, though. The only room the B and B had left has a pretty steep rate."

He pulled the glass from his lips without drinking and set it on the weathered wooden table beside the Adirondack chair she'd offered him when she'd gone inside. "A bed-and-break-fast? In town? Over ten minutes away?"

Settling into a chair on the other side of the small table, Paige shrugged. "More like fifteen with it being tourist season, although traffic didn't seem too bad this morning when we were—"

"No." The word was simple and firm, as though he'd made up his mind and there would be no argument.

She'd been afraid of this and was ready to fight. "I'm sorry? What are we saying *no* to?"

"Someone came onto your property and did a very good job of both scaring and injuring you. Then they came back this afternoon. You and Daniel are both fortunate you weren't hurt worse." He reached for the water and picked it up as though he was done with the conversation. "I'm staying here."

Digging her teeth into her tongue, Paige held back the words she wanted to speak and simply waited. Reece had never responded well to emotional arguments. He was a thinker and a planner. Emotional outbursts only put the peg in his stubborn meter and made him more unwilling to give. If she was going to keep him from bunking here, she'd have to come up with a really good reason why the idea was bad.

If she'd been thinking clearly, she'd have made a plan. She'd have known from the start he wouldn't take to the whole staying-in-town idea.

He sipped his water, watching her over the rim of the glass. He knew she knew him. He knew what she was thinking. Likely, he was eight steps ahead of her.

Back in the day, he'd always been the logical one while she'd let her emotions charge off with her mouth. He'd won every argument.

Well, he'd won every argument until she'd learned that, when she was on the losing side, all she had to do to end the showdown was kiss him.

She turned her face away from him as heat crept into her cheeks. When she composed herself and turned back, he was staring at the ice in his glass.

Seemed he hadn't forgotten about that tactic either.

Clearing her throat, Paige forced herself to relax. "You planning to sleep in your truck with Maverick then?"

"If need be." He exhaled loudly and, resting the glass on his knee, looked her straight in the eye. "Paige, despite the past, I need you to be safe."

It was the closest he'd come to acknowledging the pain she'd caused him. He probably thought she was a horrible person. Had probably spent years hating her for the way she'd left his place one night and had never returned. For the way she'd married Noah within a couple of weeks of leaving him behind.

He didn't know she'd picked up a pregnancy test on the way to her apartment that last evening. He didn't know the test had yielded an undeniable plus sign.

He also didn't know his brother had showed up on her doorstep while she was holding the test and reeling with the shock. He'd had two of his frat boy friends with him. Drunk and looking for trouble, they'd tried to force their way into her apartment.

Only the fact that Mr. Buchanan, who'd lived across the hall, had stepped out to see about the noise, had kept her from finding out their intentions.

It hadn't been the first time Quentin Campbell had made an advance. She'd had to fend him off on more than one occasion, but that night he hadn't been alone. That night had frightened her.

The next day, she'd learned that, even in his inebriated state, he'd recognized what she'd been holding in her hand.

And he'd told his mother.

The woman had never liked Paige. Had never been welcoming to Paige. It was like every made-for-TV movie she'd ever seen where the rich, golden boy's family had high aspirations for him and paid the girl to leave.

Unlike the movies, Paige had taken the money and run.

She had been terrified of Quentin Campbell and his escalating advances. Horrified by Tabitha Campbell and her utter loathing. As Reece's mother extended a check worth more than Paige had ever seen in her lifetime, every word of the other woman's scathing speech had hit home with deadly force. *You'll never be welcome... Reece will resent you... You're so worthless, even your own mother didn't stay...*

There'd been no dream future for her with Reece. If she'd married him, trouble would never end. He'd lose his family, and she knew too well how that felt in the wake of her father's death and her mother's abandonment. The best she could do for the child she'd learned about the evening before was to take the check. She'd done so silently, damming up her tears until she'd closed her apartment door behind Tabitha Campbell.

Nearly six years later, the money rested in

the same account she'd deposited it into less than a week later. No matter how much Howling Moon needed the money, it was Hailey's, the only "gift" she'd ever receive from her grandmother.

It would all go away if Tabitha Campbell found out Paige was sitting beside Reece. Somehow, as she'd threatened, she'd take the money and leave Hailey with nothing. No father. No family. No future.

Desperate, Paige had run to Noah Bristow, the only other friend she'd ever trusted, and told him everything. He'd wanted to contact Reece. She wouldn't let him.

When he'd dropped the bombshell about having the gene for Huntington's disease, she'd offered to stay and help with the kind of rescue she'd always dreamed of running. When he'd drowned, he'd just begun to show symptoms of the illness that would eventually rob him of his cognitive and motor skills.

Their friendship had been strong, although there had been no romance to their marriage. Noah had been too aware of the futility of his future and Paige had been too afraid to love again.

"Paige?" Reece's voice broke through her memories. When she looked up, he was watching her. "I said your name about six times. You okay?"

"Thinking about Noah."

A shadow crossed Reece's face, one almost worse than the hurt she'd imagined so many times in the past. She'd married Noah so quickly, Reece had to think she'd been cheating on him all along. She could never tell him differently. At this point, it might be kinder to let him believe awful things about her.

That included, when he ultimately discovered she had a daughter, letting him believe Hailey was Noah's child.

"I was surprised when you told me he was gone."

"It was a shock to everyone." She picked at a cuticle, unable to look Reece in the eye. "He was an experienced rafter, had even talked about opening a school someday, if Howling Moon ever got onto its feet and we could hire more help. I'm still not sure how it happened." The river had been high, but it was nothing Noah hadn't handled before. It was possible his physical symptoms had been worse than he'd let on, leaving him to a deadly struggle with the elements. "Four of the wolves had gotten out through a hole in the enclosures. At the time, we thought it was something they'd dug up or busted through, but now I wonder."

"You wonder if someone deliberately gave them an escape route?"

Paige nodded slowly. "If they did, then their actions led to Noah's death. He capsized on the rapids and was found almost a mile downstream from where the boat went over. It was rocky. He… He hit his head." Emotion choked the words. She'd shed tears plenty of nights. While they hadn't been husband and wife in every sense of the word, he'd been the rescuer who had provided for her when she'd had nothing. Her best friend. Her partner.

"All the more reason for me to stay here and watch over things. Whoever this is knows they're responsible for Noah's death, and it hasn't stopped them. There's no evidence of remorse, and now they're escalating." Reece shifted in his seat, seemed to be uncomfortable and moved again. He stood and paced the short distance to the railing, where he planted his hands and stared across the yard at the enclosures. "I'll be staying on the property tonight."

Paige sank against the chair, defeated. There was nothing she could say to change his mind.

If she was being honest with herself, he was right. It was dangerous for anyone to be alone with a brazen assailant who struck without warning.

Still, even with Reece present, there was danger. She could lose more than Howling Moon before this was over.

She could lose everything.

FIVE

Thunder rumbled in the distance as Reece and a leashed Maverick hiked down the slope toward the house. They'd walked the perimeter of the property then doubled back and checked the fence line around the enclosures. It had taken a couple of hours, but everything was sound. Whoever had reinforced the area where the animals were housed had done the job right.

Now he was tired, hot and hungry. The ham sandwich Paige had made before he'd set out had barely filled the hole from missing lunch. At seven? Well, he was almost hungry enough to dig into the treats he carried for Maverick.

Almost.

When he got back to the house, he was going to order pizza. Surely someone delivered.

Thunder rumbled again, closer this time, and he and Maverick picked up the pace. Out here under the tall fir trees was not the place to be with a storm rolling in.

By the time they broke into the clearing, dark clouds had thickened overhead. Paige stood on the porch. When she saw them, she cupped her hands around her mouth. "You'd better hurry into the house. There's hail coming."

Into the house? Reece looked down at Maverick, who trotted dutifully at the end of his leash. "Guess she relented on making us sleep in the truck, huh?" He scratched his partner behind the ears as they crossed the driveway. Behind them, even Paige's hybrids had taken shelter.

It was going to be a bad one then. Animals tended to know what was coming better than people did.

After a quick stop at the truck to grab his duffel and Maverick's backpack, he took the stairs two at a time and met Paige at the top. She ushered them in as a gust of wind shook the trees and rain dropped as though tipped out of a bucket.

"That was close." She shut the door then ran her hands down the legs of her jeans. It was a nervous tic, one he'd seen plenty of times whenever his mother had been around.

His mother had never made it easy on Paige,

who had spent several months living out of her car in high school after her own mother had abandoned her. Somehow, his mother had seen that as a moral failure on Paige's part.

Yet she'd failed to see the colossal failings in her youngest son. Her self-centered focus on her image and her standing in the community at the expense of justice and of innocent women like Paige was one of many reasons Reece's contact with her was almost nonexistent.

When Reece looked at Paige, he saw a woman who'd gone above and beyond to finish high school with honors and to make her way to college. He'd admired her fight and strength. They were things he'd loved about her.

He unleashed Maverick and let him sniff around the place. From her spot on a bed in the corner, Luna lifted her head to watch. The two had sailed through introductions earlier in the afternoon and seemed to get along well.

Scanning the room, Reece tried not to be obvious about his perusal of Paige's home. The spacious room was open from one end to the other. A long island separated the kitchen from the living area. Large windows set into dark wood walls brought in light, even in the midst of the storm. A closed door on the other side of the room likely led to a hallway and the bedrooms. The furniture was straight out of the eighties, as were the kitchen appliances.

Everything was slightly worn, but it was comfortable and clearly well-loved. This was a home, and he could appreciate that. While the house he'd grown up in had been artfully redecorated nearly every year, it had felt cold and slightly empty. This? This was the kind of place a man could kick off his boots and live in.

And a man had. A man who wasn't him.

He shoved his boots under the bench, shaking off anger he hadn't felt in years.

No, not anger. Hurt. Still the hurt, even after so much time had passed.

Pulling his backpack closer, he set out Mav's bowl and filled it with food, then took his water dish to the kitchen.

Paige had pulled out a chair at the sizable kitchen table. "I had some store-bought crust and made a pizza. It's on the bar."

"You read my mind." For the first time, he could smell the cheese, tomato and pepperoni. After taking care of his partner, he grabbed a piece and ate it standing at the bar. Paige had remembered his favorites, and the pie was covered with pepperoni, onions and peppers. It was odd how well she knew him when, in essence, they were now strangers. Yet another thing tweaking his emotions.

He was hungry, nothing more. Hungry and frustrated with a lack of evidence and too many possible suspects.

Stacking several slices onto the plate Paige had left on the counter, he grabbed a glass of water and sat at the end of the bar closest to Paige, who had stacks of papers scattered across the kitchen table and was working at her laptop. A plate with a half-eaten slice of pizza had been shoved to the side, almost as though she'd started eating then forgotten to finish.

She didn't seem inclined to start a conversation.

Reece devoured another slice then pulled out his phone and opened his email. He'd been out of touch most of the day, and there was no telling what he'd missed. He scrolled through a couple of random messages but stopped at one from Michael Bridges, the special agent in charge at the Denver office of the FBI, the man who could put either the gas or the brakes to the future of the RMKU.

Scanning the email, Reece nodded in agreement. Bridges was assigning special agent Liam Grey to assemble a task force to hunt down a serial killer who had been on the unit's radar for quite some time. Targeting blond women who were hiking or camping in the Rocky Mountains, the killer seemed to strike at random. Since his hunting ground spanned several states, a dedicated FBI team might help them catch him before he killed again.

Reece set the phone aside and stared at the window above the kitchen sink. Since Paige had dark hair, he didn't have to worry about the serial killer targeting her on top of whatever else was happening at Howling Moon.

And what was happening to him… Seeing Paige again had raised grief and anger he hadn't realized he still harbored. They needed to talk.

He just didn't know how to start the conversation. He polished off another half slice before he came up with the lamest opening line of his life. "You look busy."

A clap of thunder shook the house from a nearby lightning bolt.

Paige jumped and, instead of responding, picked up her phone, made an odd face and appeared to send a text. She stared at the screen for a moment, typed again then set it aside. "I'm sorry. What?"

"I said you look busy." Reece shoved in another bite of pizza. The more he ate, the hungrier he felt.

Paige sighed and shuffled some papers into a stack. She rested her elbows on the table and kneaded her temples, glancing at her phone when another pop of thunder rattled the windows. "I'm searching all of the grants I can find." She picked up her phone, made another strange face and then set it down again.

He knew all about grants. Even well funded, the RMKU still relied on grants from various organizations to put them over the top, especially when it came to care for the K-9s.

Running a nonprofit animal refuge seemed to take more than he'd imagined, and Paige was doing it all alone. "Things are that bad?"

She hesitated, closed the laptop and looked in his direction, though her eyes never met his. "We have some donors from around the country who 'adopt' the animals, but the money only goes so far. There's food and upkeep and Daniel's salary. Insurance. Taxes. Even though Seb does a lot for free, meds cost money. We also have to live. I have to find a way to keep Hailey and me fed as well." Her shoulders rose along with her deep inhale. "It's a lot."

With no outside job, Paige's life was poured into her rescue animals. It was no wonder her home didn't seem to have been updated since Reagan was president. But… "Who's Hailey?"

Her gaze shot to him then away, as though the question surprised her. Stacking a napkin on top of her plate, she stood and walked across the kitchen, where she tossed the trash into a can under the sink. "Hailey is my daughter."

The giant hunk of pizza he'd bitten off stuck in his throat. He managed not to make it obvious and grabbed his water before literally choking. Paige and Noah had a kid? He should have done his homework before he'd hit the road, but he'd been so rushed to get moving...

He glanced around the room, taking in things he would have noticed earlier if he hadn't been so fixated on his own emotions. Crayon drawings of a three-person family and of the rescues on the ranch covered the older white refrigerator. On the unfinished wood mantel above the massive stone fireplace, framed pictures stood in a row. Paige with a little girl who looked like someone had cut and pasted toddler Paige into the scene. Noah with the same little girl. The little girl with Luna and Paige. Always Paige or Noah with the child.

Not a single photo of Paige and Noah together.

He wiped his mouth on a paper towel and shoved his plate aside, appetite gone. He wouldn't read too much into that. "Where is Hailey now?"

Paige bustled around the kitchen, putting leftover pizza into storage containers and into the fridge. Wiping invisible spots off the counter. So much motion. "She's with Seb and his wife. With everything happening, I felt better if she—" Thunder echoed off the nearby mountains and rolled against the house like a crashing tidal wave. Another weird face while she looked at her phone. This time, with her eyes crossed.

What was she doing? The phone had her attention and it was...weird. "Paige?"

"Sorry." Shoving the phone into her hip pocket, she raised her eyebrows as her cheeks pinked. "Hailey hates thunderstorms ever since Noah died, so we make silly faces at the clouds whenever one rolls in. She's texting me photos."

Ah. "She has Seb's phone?"

"Lacey's."

Poor kid. "I always hated thunderstorms when I was young. Used to hide under the bed with Ranger." The dog had been a trooper, letting Reece tug his golden Lab self under the tall bed in his brother's room.

Things were so much different then.

"Hmm." Paige stopped her frenetic kitchen cleaning and tossed the rag at the sink. It missed and landed on the floor, but she didn't seem to notice. "I think I'll go to my room. I haven't slept well the past couple of nights and—" It was almost like she forgot what she was saying as she crossed the living room.

He couldn't let her leave. They needed to clear the air, talk about the past. It kept creeping into his thoughts and muddying his ability to reason. If they didn't stop dancing around why she'd left him, he might miss something.

And missing something might get Paige killed.

No. She couldn't wait. Couldn't stop. If she stayed in Reece's presence much longer, she'd blurt the truth. Conversations about Hailey were off limits. She'd said more than she wanted to earlier, but there was no rewind button. There was no way she could lie and say Hailey was Noah's. Nor could she deny her daughter was Reece's if he asked.

If she stalked to her room and hid, he'd be suspicious. It was his job to notice details and to suspect people of wrongdoing.

Still, she owed him some sort of explanation for leaving him. Some sort of apology.

Her eyes slipped shut, and she turned her face toward the ceiling. If Reece wanted to talk, she'd have to drive the conversation, because he couldn't discover the truth.

With a heavy sigh, she texted Lacey to say she was stepping away from the phone. The storm had nearly passed, so Hailey should be easy to distract. Paige had ached to be with her sweet girl during the crashing weather, knowing how much she hated it, but the novelty of sending selfies back and forth seemed to have done the trick.

So did Seb's promise of a pony ride once the storm moved on. That girl loved the miniature ponies Seb's parents raised on an adjoining piece of property.

"Paige?" Reece's voice drew her back into the room and the twisting, thorny path of the conversation they needed to have with one another.

Because whether she told him the story or not, there was definitely one thing she needed to say.

She stepped away from the hall door and shoved her phone back into her pocket. Once she was in the room, she shifted from foot to foot. Sit or stand? Inside or outside? How did you start a conversation *about* the man you'd once loved *with* the man you'd once loved? How did you say you were sorry without telling exactly *why* you were sorry?

She twisted her hair around one hand then let it fall, staring at her feet.

"I'm not going to yell or—" Reece paced to the window overlooking the animal enclosures. "Or treat you the way your father did when you did something he didn't like."

The low thread of understanding bent something in Paige's spirit. She sank to the raised hearth, staring at Reece's back. He knew her so well, down to her deepest secrets... Or at least the ones not involving him. He knew about the verbal abuse her father had heaped upon her. The complacency of a mother who'd never defended her and had ultimately abandoned her.

He knew how his mother's words so often brought back that pain. So many times he'd defended her. Had tried to understand.

They'd started dating during the high school year Paige had spent living in her car after her father had died and her mother had simply vanished. Reece had always been her friend, but in their senior year he'd taken notice of what was going on and started bringing her breakfast every morning before school. Those early morning car picnics turned into deeper conversations until they were inseparable. All the way through college, they'd been together. Had planned a future.

Until his brother and his mother drove the wedge too deep.

Now Reece was in her living room, still knowing her better than anyone—including Noah—ever had. The depth of his pain was obvious in the way he stood with his hands in his pockets and his shoulders squared.

Even Maverick picked up on it. The German shepherd rose from his bed near the door and walked to Reece, leaning into his leg the same way Luna sometimes leaned into hers when she sensed Paige was tense or upset.

All of this pain was her doing. She rubbed her hands on her knees, her blue jeans soft against her palms. "I'm sorry."

She'd barely whispered the words, but they'd clearly landed. Reece's posture softened as his eyes searched the ceiling. It was a long time before he spoke, and the distant rumbles from the receding storm rolled through the silence. "Why?"

Not *why* was she sorry. *Why* had she left.

When his mother had bought Paige's silence, she'd extracted two promises from Paige. *You are never to tell my son about this child. You will never contact him again. If you do, I will make sure you lose not only the child but everything you own. How dare you proposi-*

tion Reece's brother? You're despicable. The Campbell family had that kind of power, too. Reece's mother, a tort attorney whom judges and opposing attorneys feared, was the type of woman who buried the competition in court. She could definitely manipulate the system to wreck Paige.

It was ironic, really.

Quentin had sprawled in an armchair behind his mother, smirking, watching his vengeful lies play out in front of him as though it were a personal theater production staged for his entertainment. *You turned me down again, let's see how it works out for you.*

She could never tell Reece. He'd loved his younger brother and would never believe the truth. Her story would sound like sour grapes. After this many years had passed, it would be an unprovable accusation.

She blew her bangs out of her eyes and aimed left of the bull's-eye. "I was scared." It was true. There was no telling what Quentin would have done had she stayed.

"Of me?" Reece faced her and walked into the center of the living room, his hazel eyes bright with questions and pain. "Of the future? You should have come to me. We talked about everything, Paige. I went to pick up and you were…" He threw his hands into the air and let them drop to his thighs with a slap. "You were gone."

Her mouth was so dry. She drew her tongue along her lower lip. This was the conversation she shouldn't even be close to having. She shoved to her feet and backed toward the hall door, pinning her gaze to his, begging him to stop asking questions, to accept her apology and to understand how much leaving him had hurt her, how much knowing she'd hurt him caused her pain every single day of her life. "I'm so sorry." The words choked on the sob she hadn't felt coming.

When he stepped toward her, she raised her hands and backed up another step. "I'm sorry." She turned and fled, Luna on her heels, shutting the hall door behind her, a barrier between them. She ran to her room and crawled across her bed, burying her face in the pillow. Tears over Reece poured out like they hadn't flowed in years.

That had been more disastrous than even her worst nightmares could have imagined.

Up the hall, Reece called to Maverick and the house shook as he slammed the door and his boots pounded down the outside steps. She wouldn't blame him if he packed up and left, but there was no sound from outside. His truck remained silent. Knowing him, he was prowling the property, thinking, doing his best to bring his emotions into line. Whenever he was angry or frustrated, or even overly happy, Reece took to the outdoors to find his center. He always had.

Paige flopped onto her back and wiped the tears from her cheeks, staring at the ceiling. If only she could tell him the truth.

If she did, Hailey would lose her college fund and maybe even her mother. Reece didn't deserve to have his family's dirty laundry dumped in front of him. Not when so much time had passed.

Luna padded over and hopped onto the bed, laying down with her back pressed tightly to Paige's side. It was one of her offers of comfort. *Hug me. I can handle whatever is hurting you.*

Rolling onto her side, Paige buried her face in Luna's thick neck fur. "What would I do without you, girl?"

Luna wiggled her back until she was even tighter against Paige. *You'd be lonely.*

Yes, she would.

She lay there for a while, watching the shadows deepen as she alternated between storms of tears and bouts of emptiness.

As the darkness became complete, a howl arose from the enclosures. Almost immediately, another followed.

Paige sat up, staring at the faint moonlight pouring through the window. The animals tended to get restless after a storm had passed, as though they needed to burn off energy after taking shelter, but something felt too much like the other night, when Camelot was targeted.

Only this time, Reece and Maverick were out there too.

Maybe the pack was simply reacting to the presence of those two, but the tension in her gut demanded she check on the animals in her care. While Daniel insisted on returning as soon as possible, he'd never stayed overnight. The refuge and the animals were her responsibility.

She rolled to the side of the bed and stood, looking Luna in the eye. "Stay." That rarely worked, but maybe this time her friend would listen.

When Luna started to rise, Paige slipped out the door and closed it behind her. She couldn't risk Luna getting hurt if there was truly something dangerous going on outside.

Easing the hall door open, Paige scanned the darkened living room. No one had turned on any lights, and the trees waving in the post-storm breeze danced strange shadows across the room.

She stepped through the door, her feet padding on the hardwood. "Reece?"

No answer. He was probably still outside pacing off his pain. Likely, his agitation had the animals spun up.

Another howl sent a shudder down her back. It was entirely too dark in here.

Wrapping her arms around her waist, she hurried across the room to the couch and the light on the end table. It would be better if she had—

A heavy weight slammed her from the side and drove her into the wall.

Paige screamed as a picture frame shattered against her shoulder, broken glass slicing pain into her skin. She tried to pull free, but a hand gripped her biceps and hurled her to the floor.

A hulking figure loomed over her, a dark shadow against the dim moonlight. His face was covered with a dark mask, and he was holding something in his hands. He knelt, straddling Paige's stomach.

She screamed, but a pillow clamped down tight over her face and choked the sound. She thrashed and tried to find air, but there was no relief.

Her hands flailed, her finger slamming into the heavy stone hearth in front of the fireplace.

As her lungs burned with the frantic need for air and her pulse pounded in her ears, she dug and clawed at the stones, trying to reach the fireplace poker or the ash shovel. Something... Anything... She had to fight...

For Hailey...

For...

SIX

Reece took the outside stairs two at a time, the house shaking with each footfall.

On his heels, Maverick panted, keeping up easily with his long strides.

That was a scream. Paige's scream.

There was no denying the sound, even though he'd been near the barn when the distant screech had reached his ears. The rescues raised another howl, this one more frantic, almost as if they could hear the terror in his breathing and in Paige's cry.

He stretched for the doorknob, but the door was already partially open.

Something fell inside and there was a feeble pounding on the floor as though a struggle was coming to an end.

It could not be coming to an end.

Unable to judge what was happening in the darkness, he said a quick prayer for protection and burst into the room with no idea what he would face on the other side.

Maverick barked twice, awaiting a command.

There was nothing for him to do. While he was trained to protect Reece in certain circumstances, he wasn't trained to attack on command and would likely get hurt going in now.

It was dark in the house, and Reece's eyes weren't yet adjusted when a shadowed figure dressed in black shoved him aside and raced out the door, pounding down the steps and into the night.

He dashed inside, Maverick behind him, and tried to get his bearings in the darkness. Where was the light?

From up the hall, Luna whined and pawed at what was probably Paige's bedroom door.

Drawing his sidearm, Reece felt by the door until his fingertips brushed a switch, flooding the room with light.

Paige lay on her back by the fireplace, gasping for air, a pillow gripped tightly in white knuckles and pressed to her stomach.

"Search." He commanded Maverick to sniff out something, doubting he'd find blood but knowing he'd raise an alert if he came across an intruder.

Holstering the pistol, Reece dropped to his knees beside Paige and scanned her from head to toe as his heart tried to pound through his rib cage. She seemed to be unharmed, but her face was an alarming shade of red. "Talk to me, Paige. Are you okay?"

"I don't…know." The words were airy and came between heaving gulps of air. "Guy tried to…" She lifted the pillow slightly and let it fall. It slid from her stomach to the floor.

The man had tried to snuff the life out of Paige with a pillow? This was a whole new kind of anger. Who was doing this? Why were they coming after a woman who gave selflessly to the creatures she served?

Easing an arm behind her back, he helped her sit up. She curled into his chest, her head tucked beneath his chin, her shoulders rising and falling with each breath.

Against every ounce of his better judgment, Reece wrapped his arms around her and held her close, rocking slightly and biting back the comforting words that automatically wanted to pour out. *I've got you. I'll protect you. I won't let anyone hurt you.*

They were things he'd said to her in the past. In high school when someone had spread the truth of her living situation throughout the senior class… In college when his mother had been particularly mean…

It was no longer his place to protect her. At least, not from his heart. No, the only protection he could offer to her now was out of his duty as a law enforcement officer.

And maybe a little bit as an old friend.

Gradually, her breaths came more evenly, but she didn't pull away, even when Maverick passed them and sat next to the wall in alert stance. If there wasn't a person in the room, whatever Mav had found could wait.

Reece couldn't decide if it was minutes or hours that they sat there, Paige's familiar weight resting against him. Once again, he battled the looping of past over present, the compression of time making it seem as though she'd just been his and he'd been hers yesterday. Making it feel as though she was his to protect and to love. As though six years hadn't passed.

As though she hadn't been married to someone else in the years between.

He straightened slightly, shifting away from her until she pulled back and sat on her own.

Drawing her knees to her chest, she wrapped her arms around her legs then winced and looked away from him.

This wasn't about him, it was about her and

the threat to her life. He had no right to let the past keep him from doing his job today. Even if her earlier apology and her refusal to discuss why had gutted him nearly as much as her original disappearing act.

No. Now was not the time. "What's wrong?"

"I cut my arm." She jerked her chin toward the wall, where an empty nail indicated the spot where a picture had hung.

On the floor, Maverick sat beside a broken picture frame, several of the glass shards dark with blood. Reece rose to sit on his heels and leaned around Paige. Her gray shirt was torn at the back of her shoulder, and blood seeped into the material.

There was only one way that could have happened. He struggled to keep his breathing even. "He threw you against the wall?"

When Paige nodded, Reece snatched his phone from its holster and pressed 9-1-1.

Paige's hand on his wrist stopped him. "Don't."

"Why not?" There was no way to keep the frustration from his voice. This was ridiculous. "That sheriff needs to get out here—"

"And do nothing?"

"You were assaulted. Again." The words punched the air with enough force to make Paige's chin set in defiance.

"I've been fighting the battle longer than you have, Reece." The defeat in her voice was more heartbreaking than anything else he'd dealt with since her initial phone call.

Yesterday felt like weeks ago.

She pressed her fingers to the wound and set her expression into calm determination. "Seb will stitch me up. It won't be as pretty as an ER doc's work, but it will suffice." She widened her eyes in a *don't even think about it* look to keep him from interrupting. "Every call to the sheriff becomes one more mark in the long list of reasons for the county to close down the refuge. Now it's not just the animals who are a danger. I'm attracting the wrong sorts of people, raising the crime rates. I can hear them now, talking about how my calls to the department have made a wreck of our crime statistics."

"*You're* wrecking their stats? The sheriff is investigating a murder. There's a serial killer running around the Rocky Mountains. What's happening here is—"

"A what?" Her voice pitched up, this time with a touch of fear that had been missing before.

"Nothing. No one's been killed here." He'd looked into the sheriff's murder investigation. The victim was a middle-aged man, nothing like the RMKU's serial killer's victims. "What's Seb's number? Let's get you taken care of. Once he gets here, Mav and I will see what we can find outside."

She rattled off the number and tried to get up, but he wouldn't let her. Instead he handed her a couch cushion and had her lean against the fireplace hearth, wanting Seb to get a good look at her first.

He still didn't agree with her insistence not to call for help, but he had more resources at his disposal than any town sheriff ever would, and he was about to set them into motion. Once he got off the phone with Seb, he was going to call the sergeant's assistant, Jodie Chen, and have her get the ball rolling on background checks on every single person who had come into contact with Paige or the refuge, including the sheriff and his son-in-law.

As much as he hated it, he'd dig into Paige and Noah as well, because something told him this story ran deeper than any off them imagined.

"You had better be counting your blessings this wasn't worse." Seb pulled rubber gloves from his hands and dropped them into a plastic bag on one of the kitchen chairs. He started to gather the supplies he'd used to put a row of seven stitches in Paige's shoulder.

At the bar, Reece sat on a stool, absently scratching Luna behind the ear and staring at the window behind Paige. The curtains were drawn against the dark night, but he seemed to find the red-and-green-plaid fabric fascinating. His expression was grim, his lips tight and his eyebrows drawn into a deep V. He had said very little since Seb arrived.

"Paige, listen to me." Seb stopped stuffing his equipment into his bag. "If that glass had punctured instead of sliced, then—"

"It didn't, and whatever you were about to say didn't happen either, so we're not going to play the what-if-it-had game." Paige slid her chair a couple of inches away from Seb. Not enough to be out of reach, but enough to make her point. It was all she could do to keep panic from overtaking her. Her stomach still quaked, and she didn't need those tremors making their way out. She wanted to stuff the evening's experience into a dark closet and pretend it had never happened. "Now, I'm out of ibuprofen and I'm really hoping you have some with you. If not, I'll take whatever horse tranquilizer you have on hand."

"Very funny. I can't legally hand you drugs

meant for animals and you know it." With an exasperated exhale, Seb finished cleaning up then reached into his duffel bag and handed her a bottle of ibuprofen. "Lacey, however, believes in being prepared for my aches and pains along with the animals I'm treating."

"Thanks." Paige popped two pills dry before Seb could hand her a water bottle, which she gratefully drained when the pills stuck in her throat.

He shook his head, the silent signal he wasn't approving of her current behavior. They'd been friends since the day she'd met him at her courthouse wedding to Noah. Seb and Lacey knew her better than most people, but even they didn't know the truth about Hailey.

On the flip side, she knew Seb pretty well too. Past experience said he was about to lecture her on taking care of herself. Well, she'd put a stop to that. "How's Daniel?" Likely, Seb didn't know she'd already talked to Daniel, who'd assured her he was fine and would be back at work the next day.

His eyes darkened. "Had a decent cut on the back of his head, but no stitches. Nothing showed up on the scans. They sent him home with instructions to rest and load up on ibuprofen." With a loud exhale, he leaned closer.

"I don't like what's going on here. Maybe you should stay with Lacey and me."

"Bring all of this closer to you? To the one place where I know Hailey is safe?" Paige pulled back from him. "No." She needed to know Hailey was safe, and she'd never be able to live with herself if whoever was wreaking havoc on her property followed her to menace those she loved. It was awful enough that Daniel had been caught in the cross fire.

Seb looked as though he was about to say more, then stopped. Instead, he slid his bag across the table, away from him and turned to Reece. "Where that cut is, she's not going to be able to see it well. Keep an eye on it for her and if it starts to look infected, get her to urgent care even if you have to throw her over your shoulder and haul her there while she assures you the whole time she's fine."

"Yes, sir." For the first time, Reece turned his attention away from the window to Seb. "If it gets infected, she won't have time to argue before I have her at a doctor's office."

Paige rolled her eyes. "I know what I'm doing. Also, I'm sitting right here." It was a whole lot easier to focus on the men treating her like a child than it was for her to think about what might have happened if Reece hadn't heard her scream. She leaned to the side to put her face in Seb's line of vision, her newly minted stitches pulling tight against the back of her arm, below her shoulder. That sting wasn't going away any time soon. "I trust you. You can handle any—"

"I'm a veterinarian. You have to see a real *human* doctor eventually."

He could preach all he wanted, but the only two doctors in Crystal Ridge were Brody Carson's wife and cousin. While she had no doubt they'd treat her with exceptional medical care, her reception would be frostier than a December mountain night.

Seb slid his chair from the table and grabbed his bag. "I'm done, so I think I'll head back to the house." He leaned forward and gently hugged Paige, careful not to jostle her wounded shoulder. "Either Lacey or I will check on you tomorrow."

"I'll be fine. I promise." Paige watched him go, but she jumped when his cell phone trilled as he stepped out onto the porch and shut the door behind him.

"You are not *fine*." Reece's voice was hard.

"I will be." Her voice snapped with the same energy as the lightning had earlier. Who was he to tell her whether or not she was fine? He had no idea what she'd overcome or what she'd given up when she'd left him. Those dark days had strengthened her in ways he'd never understand.

Okay, so maybe she shouldn't be the one with the attitude here, given the secret she harbored. "I'm sorry."

"Same." Reece scrubbed his hand down his cheek. "Seb and I weren't being fair to you a while ago. You're a grown woman. But…" When he tilted his head, his eyes caught hers. The lines around the edges were deep with something Paige might have called *fear* if Reece was any other man.

But he wasn't. He was Reece Campbell. She'd never once seen him afraid. If he was afraid now, then everything was worse than even her spinning mind could imagine. She gathered what was left of the trash on the table and stood, walking past Reece to dump it in the can beneath the sink.

He caught her wrist as she passed the stool where he sat. "We have to do something different."

"Like what? Never let me out of your sight?" The thought of being with him twenty-four hours a day both drew and repelled her. There was a part of her that had never let him go. But that part had bowed to protecting Hailey's future.

"No." His grip tightened slightly as he drew her closer, until her hip brushed his knee. "If you hadn't managed to scream tonight and I hadn't been close enough to hear it—"

"I already told Seb we weren't going to play the what-if game." Her mind was doing enough of that.

"Part of my job is to play that game. To walk through what could have happened and what might happen next. Every time I walk through what happened this evening, I get stuck." He reached for her other hand, turning her to face him. "I could have lost you for good."

"Don't say that." She wanted to shout, but the words eked out on a whisper. If he'd lost her then Hailey would have lost her too. Her daughter would have been an orphan...or so everyone would believe.

When Reece drew her one step closer so she stood between his knees, the room tilted. Fear from the violence and the sudden nearness of the only man who had ever fully held her heart swirled through her, making her waver. "Please."

She wasn't sure what the *please* was for. Please don't speak? Please don't be so close? Please don't let me go?

"What did I do to make you run?" He was watching her, asking silently for the truth.

The truth she couldn't give him without wrecking everything. Once he knew, he wouldn't want her. He might join forces with his mother to take Hailey away.

Standing in front of him, so close she could see the ring of green in his hazel eyes, his mother didn't matter. The danger to her life didn't matter. Nothing else—

"Paige." The door burst open as Seb stepped into the room. "I— Whoa. Sorry."

Paige stepped back and pulled her wrists from Reece's grasp. She faced Seb, who stood in the doorway looking as though he'd walked in on them kissing—which they weren't even close to doing.

Reece stood and whistled for Maverick. "Let's go see if we can find any evidence, Mav."

The dog rose from his bed and met Reece. With a quick nod to Seb, Reece and his partner stepped into the night.

Paige couldn't stop watching until the door closed behind them. When she finally pulled her attention away, Seb was wearing an expression somewhere between amused and concerned.

"What do you need?" She dropped onto the bar stool and braced her hands on her knees.

All she wanted was to lock herself in her room and pull the heavy antique dresser in front of the door. Maybe she'd never come out.

Luna was at her side almost as soon as she sat. She dropped her head onto Paige's knee and looked up almost as if to say, *I get it. Life is hard.*

Paige pressed her forehead to her favorite creature's, closing her eyes. Whatever Seb wanted, it could wait. This was the most peace she'd felt all day, simply accepting the unconditional love of a wolf-dog who would never ask for more than she could give.

"I hate to shatter your moment, but we need to talk." Seb's voice was heavy.

Paige's head snapped up. "Is Hailey okay?"

"She's fine. Lacey's bringing her over."

Her daughter was coming home. Paige ached to hug her close, to know she was safe and—

Wait. "She can't come here. There's too much going on." She also couldn't be near her birth father.

"Joe Bishop's got a horse having a difficult birth. He needs me there now, and I need Lacey's help. We can't take Hailey with us."

No, they couldn't.

Paige had nowhere else for Hailey to go. Trusted friends in Crystal Ridge were few and far between.

She'd have to hustle Hailey to her room and stay there with her. Nothing in her was ready for Hailey to meet Reece. "I understand."

"I'm sorry, Paige. I know you don't want her here when there's so much chaos and danger. Lacey or I will come back as soon as we can in the morning and pick her up. We want her safe too."

"I know." Paige managed a smile. "You love her as much as if she were your own."

"Something tells me you're both safer with Reece than either of you would be anywhere else." Before she could speak, he jerked his thumb over his shoulder, indicating the door. "He's down by the enclosures, checking the animals. They're pacing quite a bit. I'll let him know Lacey's coming so it doesn't throw him when she pulls into the driveway." His expression grew serious. "Whatever was happening between the two of you when I walked in, it looked intense."

"It was nothing." Paige's voice was hard.

It could never be anything either, not even if her traitorous heart wondered what would happen if she confessed everything.

SEVEN

He'd waited almost too long to set Maverick to scenting the area, especially given the damp ground and earlier rainfall. But he'd been reluctant to leave Paige until he'd known for sure she wasn't badly injured.

She was safe for now, but his brain wouldn't stop spinning through everything that could have gone wrong. If he'd been thirty seconds later getting to her...

Commanding Maverick to sit, Reece leaned back against a tree at the edge of the property, the damp bark soaking through his T-shirt. Across the yard, two sets of taillights disappeared around the bend in the driveway, Seb and his wife leaving for some veterinarian emergency.

That meant Paige's daughter was in the house. Paige and *Noah's* daughter. Seeing Paige had already turned his heart backward in his chest. Learning she was a widow had shocked him further.

Seeing Paige with her daughter, knowing that, had she not run, they could have had a child together by now? That might be the very thing that did him in.

He'd known helping Paige was going to be hard, but he'd still packed up and rushed to her rescue, driven by...

Honestly, he had no idea what had driven him. Morbid curiosity? The shadows of the future they could have had?

Regardless, he hadn't anticipated seeing her would lead to the kind of confusion and pain he now felt. He'd long ago drawn a tight rein on his emotions concerning Paige. Two days ago, he'd have said she still caused him a twinge of pain every now and then, but not this kind of brutal body blow. He'd thought the hurt was long dead, that he could merely see her as a person from his past.

He couldn't. Paige Simmons was still lodged firmly in his heart, her abandonment still knifed his chest.

But her name wasn't Paige Simmons anymore. It was Paige *Bristow*.

Boy, was he tired of correcting himself.

You're here working a case, Campbell. Make

it about the case. Maybe he could make some sense of the facts since his emotions were bent on twisting with each passing moment.

Thinking about the case was no better than thinking about Paige. All he kept running up against was dead ends.

The rain had left the ground a sodden mess that made it nearly impossible for Maverick to scent anything. The few footprints at the foot of the porch stairs were shapeless and undefined. Even a trek to the logging road had proved fruitless. While there was evidence someone had parked there recently, the mud had been too wet and loose to offer up anything other than vague impressions.

Vague impressions were all he had when it came to his suspects as well. Too many people had reason to want Howling Moon shut down, but none of them had a reason to want Paige dead. Too many suspects was worse than none at all.

It was time to start narrowing them down. For that, he needed another brain, someone to bounce ideas off and to talk through theories with.

He glanced at his watch. It was after nine, but Tyson would still be up. Reece could talk through Paige's situation with his boss, maybe air some of his personal issues as well. He needed to get his emotions into open air before he made another mistake like the one he'd almost made earlier when he'd come very close to kissing Paige.

He'd been trying not to think about it. In fact, he'd been surprised by the draw to her given the way everything had ended six years earlier.

When she'd curled up in his arms and sobbed out her fear and her shock, the protective instinct he'd felt for her almost from the day he'd met her had kicked back in.

When he'd drawn her close and they'd locked eyes later... The most natural thing in the world—what had always come naturally to him—was the drive to kiss her, to remind her he was there and he was never going to leave her or hurt her.

Except those feelings were in a past reality that no longer existed. There was no longer a Reece and Paige. There was only a man named Reece living his life separately from a woman named Paige.

It felt unnatural to think of them as two separate people with two separate lives.

That was the problem.

Paige had left him and married someone else. Had a child with someone else.

Keep reminding yourself, pal. Never forget it.

Before he could fall into the rabbit hole of self-pity again, he jerked his phone from its holster and called Tyson.

It was nearly four rings before the sergeant answered. "Wilkes." His voice was tight and clipped.

Tyson only answered like that when something was wrong. "Has something happened in the Chloe Baker case?" Baby Chloe had been missing for months after the mysterious death of her mother. The team's search for the infant had consumed them.

"No. Unfortunately, there's no news." Tyson exhaled loudly. "Is everything okay on your end?"

"No. Sounds like things aren't good on your end either." They could talk about Paige's case later. The undercurrent in Tyson's tone set Reece on edge. Aside from the missing baby, there was only one other thing that would have Tyson so defeated. "Something else happened at headquarters, didn't it?" The unit had battled a series of dangerous incidents over the past few months. A training weapon had been loaded with overpacked blanks, and a keypad had been tampered with.

Worst of all, some of the dogs had vanished from the kennels, bolting when a door had been opened. Maverick had been one of those animals, and the search for his partner had taken years off Reece's life.

It was clear someone with malicious intent was targeting the K-9s.

Tyson's silence confirmed Reece's suspicions. "What happened?"

"The AC went out in the kennel and the backup generator failed."

Oh no. Had it only been two days ago when he'd stood with Harlow and listened to the machines whirr, grateful for their power in the horrendous heat plaguing Denver? "How are the K-9s?"

"Most of them are okay. Anthony Isaacs was training some of the new recruits and realized something was wrong."

"'Most of them?' Who's injured?" These were fellow officers. Partners. It was a gut punch to think any of them might be—

"Two of the trainees, Rebel and Shiloh, along with Harlow's partner Nell, were in corner kennels where the air circulation was lower. They were close to heat exhaustion, but Sydney got their temps down."

Reece dropped his head back against the tree. They were safe. Sydney Jones was an incredible veterinarian who provided the unit's K-9s with the highest level of care.

But for the unit and its backup to go bad at the same time was suspicious. "Sabotage?"

"You know what we say."

"There's no such thing as coincidence."

"I'm still at headquarters. I've got a buddy who's an HVAC tech and he's meeting me to look at the system. He'll know if something was tampered with." Tyson cleared his throat. "But I'm guessing that's not why you called."

Tyson didn't need to hear Reece pour out his guts about his ex when the team was in the middle of a crisis. "I wanted to run over some stuff with you now that I might be here a few more days. I've got Jodie running background checks that might get the ball rolling faster."

"You can't stay forever. We've got you there on a tenuous thread, investigating the shooting of a red wolf hybrid. If anyone pushes your jurisdiction, doubt it will fly."

"I know."

"I have a feeling you called me about more than the case." The strain in Tyson's voice eased, almost as though he was slipping into the role of friend.

"Nah. It's good."

"*Nah, it's good?* You sound like a middle-schooler who lost his date to the homecoming dance. What's really going on?"

"You've got other things—"

"All I'm doing is waiting. Might as well talk." Tyson chuckled. "It's harder than you thought seeing her again, isn't it?"

Tyson knew some of Reece's history with Paige, but he'd never confessed his certainty that she was *the one*, that he'd had a ring in his pocket the night she'd left.

That part hurt too much to be voiced. "It's a bit harder. But I've got two direct attacks on her and another on one of her employees." He sketched out a quick summary of the events since his arrival. "The sheriff is no help. Either he's in the hip pocket of whoever is out to shut Paige down, or the guy who's out to shut Paige down is in his hip pocket."

"Neither of those is good. Hang on." Tyson said something that was muffled, then he was back. "Look, Utley's here to look at the HVAC units. But hear me say this… Emotions have no place in investigating. You loved this woman and something inside you will always want to protect her. You have to keep the personal off the table."

Too late.

"Scratch that. You'll never be able to move

forward without answers from her. At some point, you'll have to get them if you have any chance of thinking through this case. Get honest with her. You know if you need to talk out any case details, I'm right here."

"I know. Go do your thing. Let me know what you find out."

"You've got it." Tyson killed the call.

Reece holstered his phone and stared at the back of Paige's home. Tyson was right. He needed answers, both personally and professionally.

He just wasn't sure he wanted to know what they were.

"Mama, why did Aunt Lacey and Uncle Seb have to go to the farm?"

It was yet another in a long line of questions from Hailey. Keyed up from the earlier storm and from, what was to her, a middle-of-the-night ride back to the house, she had been firing queries nonstop since she'd walked in the door with her red flannel blanket in tow.

Paige sat on the corner of the couch in the dark living room with Hailey snuggled to her chest. The little girl's hugs and questions had done more to ease the fear from earlier than anything else ever could. At the moment, she never wanted to let her daughter out of her sight again.

Given the way things were going on the refuge, Hailey would have to return to Seb and Lacey's as soon as possible. The thought of anything happening to her daughter made Paige want to pack up and drive until she ran out of gas.

"Mama?" Hailey pressed a finger against Paige's nose. "Why?"

Oh yeah. There had been another question. "Because sometimes mama animals need help to bring their baby animals into the world."

Paige braced for another why, but the answer seemed to satisfy Hailey, who snuggled her head against her mother's shoulder and pulled her little security blanket up under her chin.

That blanket… When Noah had died, Hailey had barely been old enough to understand. Searching for a way to keep alive the only father Hailey had ever known, Paige had cut one of his big flannel shirts and stitched together a way for Hailey to keep it with her always. Outside of her hours at preschool, the blanket was always with her.

Paige pressed a kiss to Hailey's hair. She missed Noah too. He'd been her best friend. Her confidant. Her partner. While they'd had separate bedrooms, their marriage had been a good one, emotionally fulfilling for them both. Noah had never wanted to risk passing his condition on to a child, and they had never shared the type of love that would make them truly husband and wife, although they'd been close. She'd walked with him as the small symptoms of his diagnosis began to crop up and he'd realized the future was coming faster than he wanted it to. He'd walked with her through the grief of leaving Reece behind and the long days and nights of raising a newborn.

Because sometimes mama animals need help to bring their baby animals into the world. Sometimes human mamas did too. Noah had been right by her side, as involved and as excited as if Hailey was his own. She was his only opportunity to love and raise a child. Over and over, he'd urged Paige to tell Reece the truth, despite the dire consequences Tabitha Campbell could dish out.

Every time she'd wavered and considered calling Reece, Paige had looked at the bank account holding her daughter's future… Had laid beside the precious girl as she'd slept and trembled with the question of whether or not Tabitha Campbell would rip her daughter away from her. With whether or not she dared to introduce her daughter to a family with a son like Reece's brother Quentin.

With whether or not Reece could ever forgive her.

Now he was here, and there was no way for her to stop whatever came next. The only thing she could do was to hold her silence. It was the one safeguard between Hailey and the fury of Reece's mother.

The house rocked gently as Reece and Maverick clomped up the stairs, and the door opened. His shadow filled the doorway, backed by the outdoor lights. In silhouette, his broad shoulders seemed even broader than usual. "Paige?" His voice was low, hesitant.

He knew Hailey was present.

Hailey's regular breathing against her chest said she'd already fallen asleep. Poor thing. She was probably wiped out from the storm and from being hauled out of bed at nine to trek back home. So much excitement for a five-year-old.

As gently as she could, fearful of waking her sleeping daughter, Paige straightened, holding Hailey close against her chest. "On the couch. Don't turn on the light."

"Are you okay?" Reece stepped across the threshold. His voice held an edge of anger and fear again, as though he worried he'd missed something and she'd paid the price.

Her heart flipped against her ribs. This had to be even harder on him than it was on her.

She knew every reason she'd left him behind. He had no idea.

She bit back yet another apology. "Everything is fine. Hailey is asleep. I don't want to wake her up." It took all of her strength to stand, and her shoulder burned and ached with the motion and with the burden of holding the slack weight of a sleeping almost-kindergartener. These days of toting Hailey around were coming quickly to an end, yet another thing dragging her feelings low. Their little girl was steadily growing up and Reece had no idea.

She'd almost made it to the hall when Reece approached. In the dim light spilling from the open door, he'd have a clear view of the child in her arms.

Paige fought the urge to turn away from him. What would he think if she did? It would cut him, make him feel like she didn't trust him with her child. Far from it. She trusted him completely. Too much.

Seeing them together was going to gut her, especially when she had to bite her tongue against blurting out the truth to protect Hailey's future and to preserve Reece's family.

Commanding Maverick to his bed, Reece met Paige at the hallway door. "Need help?"

She shook her head, unable to speak. She'd

never imagined the two of them would be in the same room together, let alone close enough to breathe the same air.

He eased back to get a look at the face against her chest. In the shadowy light, Paige couldn't read his expression, but she could definitely see his eyes when they lifted to hers. "She looks like you."

Paige nodded again. Hailey really was a little mini-me. "I have to—" She cleared her throat. "Have to get her to bed before—" *Before you look too closely and see she might look like me, but her chin and nose are all you.*

"Go ahead. Definitely wouldn't want to wake her. She's probably exhausted." He turned and walked away, going back to close the door.

Paige fled up the hall, Hailey heavier than she'd ever been. *Lord, don't let me fall.* Not onto the floor and not into the past.

Her heart hammered and her stomach roiled. Reece had looked his daughter in the face then turned and walked away with no recognition. Some deep part of her had hoped he'd see. Had hoped he'd figure out the truth without her speaking. This was all so cruel.

It was also all her fault. Was it worth the money that secured Hailey's college education? Was it worth the risk Tabitha Campbell could wrest the child from her arms? Was preserving Reece's beliefs about the love of his family worth keeping him from his daughter?

Until he'd pulled into her driveway, she'd been certain her silence was the right choice. Now?

She deposited Hailey safely in her bed, tucking her under the covers and placing a kiss on soft brown hair the exact same color as her own. Looking down at her daughter, bathed in the soft glow of a moon-shaped night-light, Paige bit back tears. It was too much, too fast. Camelot wounded. Daniel attacked. Her life threatened twice...once in her own home.

And Reece.

If only she could lock the door and crawl into bed beside her daughter, snuggle the sleeping little girl close and stay right there forever where everything was easy and they were both safe in the way things had always been.

Except the way things had always been was built on a lie. Could she keep living in a massive untruth, even one she'd never spoken aloud? Because she'd never said to anyone that Noah was Hailey's father.

People had assumed. She'd let them.

It was still a lie.

One destined to destroy Reece if he ever learned the truth.

EIGHT

Reece crept across the living room by the dim light of early morning, scrubbing his hands down his cheeks. Paige had better have coffee and it had better be easy to find. He wasn't going to survive more than ten minutes without caffeine in his system. While the couch had been surprisingly comfortable, it had made his six-foot-one frame feel like he'd landed squarely in Oz's Munchkinland.

Sleep hadn't been in abundance anyway. He was too aware of every sound outside the house, and there had been a lot of them. Between the animals pacing in the enclosures he could see from his window and the breeze twisting the trees as the front made its final passage, there had been more than enough suspicious noises to keep him on high alert.

And then there was Paige and her daughter

sleeping in their rooms down the hall. They were under his protection.

Although they weren't technically his to protect, at least not in a personal way.

That might have been the real thing plaguing him through the dark night. It felt as though he hung suspended between reality and *what might have been*. In another world, he'd be the man who had a daughter with Paige. He'd be the one sharing their lives. He'd have a right to stand between them and danger.

Seeing her with the little girl had tweaked his sense of time. It was as though his life was a book that was suddenly closed, the pages pressed tightly together. The beginning and the end butted against each other. If he was the kind of guy who let his imagination run, it would be easy to pretend the whispered moment in the darkness with the child between them was a routine part of a shared life.

He wasn't about to start daydreaming now. He'd spent half the night praying for God to help him focus and think like an investigator and not as a jilted ex. After all, he was the one who'd come when she called. If he was feeling wonky, it was his own fault.

Padding across the hardwood floor, he glanced at the pallet where Maverick had spent most of the night. The German shepherd was curled in a ball but his eyes followed Reece's every move. When no command came, he tucked his nose beneath his tail. The K-9 was as exhausted as his human partner.

It only took a minute to locate the coffeepot on the counter and to find the coffee stored above it. He had counted the fifth scoop into the filter when Maverick yipped a warning before standing and walking to the door, pressing his nose to the crack between the door and the jamb.

Reece glanced at the hall, but the house remained silent. He laid the coffee scoop on the gray Formica counter and crossed the den. Maverick could obviously sense something that hadn't reached Reece's ears.

Before he could get to the door, tires crunched on gravel as a vehicle came in fast.

He jogged across the room, Maverick meeting him halfway, then stopped and turned toward his backpack. His gun and badge were secured in a lockbox, away from any chance of Paige's daughter accidentally stumbling on either of them.

He turned back to the door. There wasn't time to dig them out and unlock the box. He'd have to face whatever was outside unarmed.

A truck door slammed. "Paige!" A man's voice roared.

Definitely no time to waste.

He was out the door and onto the high porch, Maverick at his heels, before he realized he hadn't even stopped for shoes.

The yelling began again, a barely intelligible stream of curses and accusations, all peppered with Paige's name. Noah's as well.

Reece's whole being heated as he ran down the stairs, looking over the side to assess the situation. A huge red pickup was parked at an angle in the driveway. Near the barn, a man had backed Paige against the fence and was screaming at her as he shoved a stack of papers into her face.

He hadn't realized she'd left the house.

She was even more pale than she'd been the night before as she practically did a backbend over the fence, trying to get away from the man.

Reece couldn't speak. Didn't stop to think. Hardly felt the gravel digging into his bare feet. He was across the driveway before he had a plan. His hand gripped the man's shoulder and pulled so fast that the guy stumbled backward on the gravel and went down to one knee.

Paige stepped around him and stood behind

Reece, resting a hand on his back. He could hear her breathing.

"You okay?" He never took his eyes off the blond head that faced the ground.

"Fine."

Reece knew her well enough to know she wasn't, but she would put on a brave face in front of the man who'd been screaming at her.

Resisting the urge to jerk the guy to his feet by the back of his collar, Reece balled his fists at his sides, willing himself not to go on the attack. "Get up. Now."

The man didn't move, a sheaf of papers still gripped in the fist pressed to the gravel.

"I said get up. Keep your hands away from your body."

It seemed to take hours, but the man finally shifted and stood, holding his hands out to his sides. He was even slower about turning to face Reece.

When he did, Reece's jaw tightened until his temples pounded.

Brody Carson.

Reece could feel his nostrils flare as anger rose in him. He waited a couple of deep breaths before he addressed the sheriff's son-in-law, who'd become his number-one suspect. "Do you enjoy threatening women, Mr. Carson?"

Brody tightened his expression and turned away, staring at his truck.

No way did this guy get to make a run for it, not without answering for terrorizing Paige at the crack of dawn.

What was she doing up and outside this early anyway?

It didn't matter. What did matter was him getting into investigative mode instead of *the guy who once loved Paige* mode. He forced himself to relax and unclenched his fists. "Mr. Carson, I'll ask again. What are you doing here?"

Brody's shoulders heaved as he pulled in breaths, obviously still raging with whatever anger had fueled his outburst. In the shadow of another man, he wasn't so tough.

Just like a bully, to back down when faced with someone tougher.

Clearly, Brody Carson didn't know Paige. Reece had seen her in action in her self-defense classes in college. Given the right circumstances, she could leave a guy walking with a limp for days.

Suddenly, Brody lifted the papers again and shook them. "I'm done, Paige. Done. You thought it was bad before? You haven't seen anything yet."

"What's that supposed to mean?" Stepping to the side, Reece blocked Brody's view of Paige. "What was 'bad before'?"

"She knows."

"I think you need to leave. Right now. You and I can take this conversation up later when you aren't on Paige's land threatening her." Reece took one step closer to Brody, as close as he could get to the man without actually touching him.

Brody yielded, a flicker of fear in his eyes as he looked slightly up to meet Reece's fiery gaze. As he backed off, he tossed the papers over Reece's shoulder at Paige. "You're finished here. You and your wolves."

"Leave." Reece leaned toward Brody, and the man turned and walked away.

He spun out of the drive in a hail of dirt and gravel, leaving tire tracks behind.

Paige planted her hands on her hips and stared at the damage. "Great. Now I know how I'm spending my morning."

"I'll help." Reece eyed her, searching for signs of trauma or fear.

Instead, she looked angry. With a huff, she reached down and gathered the papers Brody had hurled in her face.

Kneeling to help, Reece glanced at one of

the pages as he passed it to her. It looked like a bunch of legalese to him. "What was he so mad about?"

Everything about Paige seemed to deflate. She sank against a fence post and stared at the jumble of papers in her hands, almost as though she didn't actually see them. Whatever it was, it cut her deeply.

Something about Noah, because Brody had yelled his name more than once.

Paige dropped her head back against the post and stared at the sky. "I don't really know. I was too shocked to understand. It was something about investors pulling out because of Howling Moon." She thrust the sheets in Reece's direction so suddenly that he jumped and grabbed them to his chest. "I don't think I want to do this anymore."

"Whoa. Hey." Rolling the papers into a tube, Reece shoved them into the fence to get them out of the way then stepped in front of Paige. He rested his hands on her shoulders and bent to look her in the eye. "Don't want to do what anymore?"

She shook her head, glancing to Reece's left. "This." Her voice was tight. "This fight. This constant struggle. This clawing to hold it all together." She inhaled deeply then pinned Reece's gaze with damp eyes. "I'm scared."

The bald confession tore through Reece's professionalism for the last time. Without caring their past was a mess and she'd ripped his future into pieces, he slipped his arms around her back and pulled her closer, resting his forehead against hers. Their breaths mingled between them. "I'm here." He shouldn't promise her anything, but he was.

"I can't keep doing this."

"I'll help." He tilted his head until his lips brushed her ear. "I'm not leaving. You're safe. I'll make sure." And he would. He'd put his life between her and anybody who tried to harm her. He'd do what it took to make sure she was safe.

It was the one thing he knew for certain, standing there with her in his arms, her breath warm against his neck. It was a throwback to the past, to when they'd loved each other, had assumed they'd be each other's forever.

Past, meet present.

Her chin lifted slightly, bringing her lips so close to his.

Close enough to reclaim what they'd once shared, to—

"Mama?" The voice, thin and tinny, wedged between them.

With a gasp, Paige pulled away from him, backing into the fence as she reached for a device on her hip.

He hadn't even noticed she was wearing it.

She turned away and started walking toward the house, speaking into the device. "Are you awake, kiddo?"

The answer was muffled as her footsteps crunched on the gravel. She never looked back.

Just like she'd done six years ago.

Reece dropped against the fence and watched her as Maverick leaned against his knee. He'd almost forgotten his partner was there, the same way he'd almost forgotten the way Paige had gutted him. "I guess some lessons never get learned, huh?" He scratched the shepherd behind the ears and looked down at the K-9, but the papers he'd shoved in the fence nearly took his eye out.

He'd forgotten about those too. Now, as he pulled them free, he had a feeling he held in his hands the motive behind Paige's terror.

Paige cracked another egg into the bowl then stared down at the yolks floating there. *One… Two… Three… Twelve?*

Had she really done that? There were only three of them in the house. There was no need to scramble an entire dozen. Yet here she stood with an empty carton and twelve sunny yellow yolks staring up at her.

She grabbed the whisk, but her hand trembled and she fumbled it, watching helplessly as it bounced on the floor at her feet.

Bracing her hands on the edge of the counter, Paige closed her eyes and held on. She'd been brave too long. Strong too long. Reece's assertion that he'd protect her, he'd help her…

It had cracked something in her soul. For the first time since those initial dark weeks after Noah died, life felt too big to handle. Running the refuge… Trying to get by on pennies when she needed dollars… Raising a daughter alone…

She bore bruises on her body. An ache in her chest. Fear in her soul. Someone had injured her and Daniel… Brody Carson had made her feel as helpless as a gnat about to be crushed beneath a cowboy boot. Adrenaline had caused her to buck up to him, but fear had shuddered through her body.

Someone wanted her destroyed at best, dead at worst. They'd hurt those closest to her if they had to. Daniel's injury was proof.

The reality was inescapable and horrifying. To make everything worse, in the midst of this morning's fear, she'd fallen against Reece and had never wanted to leave. She'd felt safe. Protected. Had felt as though he'd shield her from the world.

Even more, she'd felt loved.

Loved like she hadn't felt in six years.

Like she could not feel again. Not now. Not ever.

Her whole life was falling apart. The man throwing gasoline onto an already raging inferno of disasters was outside, searching for evidence.

"Mama?" Hailey walked into the kitchen and wrapped her arms around Paige's hips. "Can I help cook eggs?"

It took all Paige had to swallow the hurricane and face her daughter with peace in her expression. Leaning down, she pressed a kiss to Hailey's upturned forehead. For the past few months, she'd been helping Paige cook, and clearly loved the help she provided. "You definitely can. Grab your step stool."

Hailey hopped away to drag over the pink plastic step she used to reach the kitchen counters, and Paige bit back a grin. She'd chosen orange shorts and a bright pink sweatshirt for her morning attire.

Well, they could all use some. Hailey was

definitely her light in the dark. She thanked God daily for the little girl who had colored her world in a whole new way.

Guilt fired through her. *Lord, have I been wrong keeping Reece from the joy of being Hailey's parent?* She avoided talking to God about Reece, afraid she wouldn't want to hear what He had to say. Now, the conversation seemed unavoidable.

Paige scooped the whisk from the floor and dropped it into the sink, grabbing the colorful one Hailey had picked out from a dollar bin when she'd started helping in the kitchen. When her hand shook, she laid the whisk beside the bowl on the counter and hoped her daughter wouldn't notice. With just the two of them, it was hard to keep the little girl from getting wind of grown-up problems. There had been enough upheaval in Hailey's life after Noah's death. She didn't need to know there was a wicked storm brewing around her now.

Forcing a smile, Paige slid the bowl in front of Hailey as she stepped up onto the stool. "You know what to do." She leaned against the counter, crossing her arms over her stomach in her usual *my hands are off* posture, letting Hailey know she had the reins.

Snatching up the whisk, Hailey aimed for the bowl then stopped. "That's a lot of eggs."

"Yeah, well…" She couldn't fess up to being distracted by present danger and past love. "Mama has an old friend here to help with the rescues and I thought we could give his dog and Luna some eggs as a treat."

With a huge grin of approval, Hailey set to work, sloshing at least two eggs onto the counter.

Paige had settled a large skillet on the stove and was reaching for the butter when the outside door opened. Her fingers froze on the handle of the pan.

Although he'd seen Hailey the night before, Reece was about to officially meet her. Would something inside him whisper, *This is your daughter*?

When she turned, Hailey had stopped whisking and was staring at Reece. One hand was still on the utensil and one on the bowl.

Reece had frozen at the door, his hand on the knob after closing it. The space between him and his daughter seemed to scream the truth so loudly, Paige was shocked she was the only one who heard it.

Without warning, Hailey dropped the whisk handle onto the side of the bowl. "I like your dog. Can I pet it?"

Reece blinked twice, as though waking up from a quick nap. "Uh, yeah. Sure." He spoke a command and Maverick sat at his side, panting.

Jumping off the stool, Hailey walked to the end of the bar, slowed her pace and crept to the dog, her hand outstretched the way Noah and Paige had taught her. She loved dogs and could be exuberant around them, so they'd had to train her to approach new friends.

Hailey stopped a few feet from Maverick and tilted her head. "I'm Hailey." She addressed the dog, not Reece.

Paige slipped to the bar to watch, her knees weak. If Reece realized Hailey's relationship to him, the truth would be out there.

A boulder would lift. She might be able to breathe again.

A whole new weight would fall into place. The weight of wrecking Reece's family and of his mother's wrath.

Crouching beside Maverick, Reece laid a hand on the dog's neck and motioned for Hailey to come closer. "This is Maverick. You can pet him if you want to. You're doing a great job introducing yourself to him."

"Mama and Pops taught me how. *Go slow. Let them sniff.*" She dipped her voice to affect Noah's deeper tone. He'd jokingly called himself Pops when she was a baby, and Hailey had picked up the moniker. It fit the joyful man who'd been her father figure.

As Hailey spoke, Maverick sniffed her hand then licked her fingers. She giggled.

That sound never failed to lift Paige's spirits. She smiled in spite of the situation.

As Hailey scratched Maverick under the chin then behind the ears, she looked up at Reece. "You're a policeman."

"How do you know that?" His voice held amusement and affection.

"Maverick has a badge on his vest. It says *K-9*. Police dogs say *K-9*."

Reece grinned. It looked so much like Hailey's smile that Paige grabbed the counter for support. How could he not see?

"Very smart." He never took his eyes off Hailey as she buried her fingers in the fur at Maverick's neck.

Paige never took her eyes off Reece. She felt hot and cold.

There was warmth watching Reece with his daughter. But it was like viewing a movie from a distance; a heartwarming family story that tugged at the heartstrings but was a complete illusion.

Then there was a chill from the truth. No

matter how sweet and innocent this little meeting appeared to be, it was fraught with deception and pain in an undercurrent that could destroy everything if its full force was unleashed.

With another laugh, Hailey dropped onto her bottom. Maverick laid beside her and thumped his head in her lap, rolling onto his back to expose his belly.

With a chuckle, Reece stood. "Well, you two made friends quickly." He looked up suddenly, catching Paige as she watched. His smile faded as he glanced down at Hailey then back to her. "Can we talk?"

NINE

He'd thought Paige's daughter looked like her when he'd seen her last night in the semidarkness, but now? The child was every ounce what he'd heard people refer to as a mini-me. Her eyes, her coloring… She was one hundred percent Paige's little girl. He struggled to find a trace of the blond hair or blue eyes he'd seen in pictures of Noah Bristow scattered around the house, but he found none.

The way Paige watched from the kitchen…

He needed to shove aside these little blasts of imagination that layered over reality. Paige was not his girlfriend or his spouse. Hailey was not his child. This was not their everyday life.

It was not their life at all.

Something about it was making Paige uneasy.

Was it the same kind of uneasiness flowing through him? He'd been angry for years until he'd forgiven her the way God asked, but that didn't take away the sting of what she'd done.

The past couple of days, being in her company though... It was making him forget the doubts and the hurt. Something about her presence was balm to the very wounds she'd inflicted. It was confusing and gut-churning, and he had no idea what to do with any of it.

As he approached, her eyebrows drew together, deepening the lines in her forehead. She tugged her lower lip between her teeth and wrapped her arms around herself, almost as though anticipating a blow.

Who could blame her? She'd taken plenty of hits in the past forty-eight hours, literally and figuratively. His words had probably only added stress to the situation. *Can we talk?* were words nobody ever wanted to hear in any situation.

He could have phrased it differently, but he hadn't been thinking. He'd just known he'd needed to tell her what he'd found outside and what he'd read in the papers shoved into his back pocket.

With another glance at Hailey and Maverick, he tipped his head toward the corner of the kitchen, where they could talk privately while still watching the little girl and his partner. Though Hailey was a natural with the K-9, and Maverick was incredibly well trained, he was still a little leery of leaving them together unattended. Even though Maverick had taken to the dark-haired little girl like he'd never attached to anyone else in his life. A cautious K-9, he rarely exposed his belly to anyone.

Seemed he was smitten with Paige's daughter.

Reece could appreciate that. The kiddo was the cutest he'd ever met.

Paige followed him to the corner near the stove, her posture and her expression radiating tension.

After her meltdown in his arms this morning, he wasn't quite sure how to handle it. What he wanted to do was to pull her close again, but that was dangerous for both of them. Not to mention it would raise all sorts of questions in Hailey. Instead, he leaned toward her. "Are you okay?"

"I…" She dug her teeth into her lip and seemed to read something in his eyes. After a beat, she pulled in a breath and dropped her arms to her sides. "There's a lot going on. What did you want to talk about?"

Nothing she wanted to hear. "I found the entry point for the guy who was in the house last night."

She nodded slowly, her face growing pale.

Leaning against the counter, she glanced at Hailey then spoke quietly. "I'm guessing the door to the garage. The one at the back of the house that you can't see from the driveway."

"You're guessing right." The door had been pried open with something, likely a crowbar. "I braced it from the inside so this can't happen again. In a bit, I'll check and make sure everything is holding." It would give him something to do so he wouldn't encroach on Paige and Hailey's time together. "I can get audible alarms. They'll go off if anyone opens a window. Inexpensive, but an easy way to possibly scare someone off if they try to enter again."

Paige nodded but she didn't relax. She looked past him at Hailey, watching her daughter giggle as she petted Maverick's belly.

That could be the problem. She might be worried about Hailey's safety with the constant threats over the past few days. Or she could simply be concerned about Maverick's temperament with a young child. Or—

"Is there…anything else?"

No, whatever was bothering her didn't seem to be concern about Maverick. Why did she sound like she was fishing for something? Or like she already knew what he had read in Brody's papers?

"How do you know there's something else?"

"Because I know you."

The low words were another punch to the gut. She did. That was a huge part of the problem.

A problem that had nothing to do with why he was there. Pulling the papers from his back pocket, he passed them to her. "This is what Brody Carson was so angry about."

"I got that when he threw them at me." She stared at the pages then looked up at him as though confused by the situation. After a long moment of studying him, she finally relaxed slightly and flipped through the papers, though he doubted she really saw what was in them. "What is it?" She looked up and shook her head. "I got zero sleep last night again and my brain it's…mush. This is legal jargon, so nothing makes sense."

So that was the source of her strange mood. Exhaustion.

Reece couldn't blame her. A man had tried to kill her in her own home. Her guard was probably so high, she'd heard every creak in the house and every rustle of the animals outside, same as he had.

Well, what he'd found in those documents wasn't going to make her feel any safer.

"It's a business agreement outlining a partnership between Brody and a company called Wild River Outdoors. Ever heard of them?"

Pursing her lips, Paige stared at her fingernails. "No, but Brody's got his fingers in every outdoor adventure business for twenty miles around Crystal Ridge. Anybody looking for a river guide or a trail guide likely books through one of his companies. He's done a pretty thorough job of wiping out the competition." A layer of bitterness coated the words.

It was so bitter he could almost taste it. "What are you not saying, Paige?" He needed to know everything if he was going to get to the bottom of this and to ensure her safety and her daughter's as well.

"Everyone knows running an animal refuge is not a moneymaker. Howling Moon is a nonprofit. We legally can't make money off of it, although we can take a salary. We barely make it as it is, so Noah and I both had to either look for grants to help us survive and run the refuge or we've had to work off-site. Up until Noah died, I worked part-time at a daycare center. He worked for a contractor that installs cable. It gave us enough to survive."

"Okay?" That didn't explain the twinge in her voice.

She sighed and crossed her arms over her

stomach. "Noah loved the outdoors. Loved helping people get more comfortable outside four walls and living in the world around them. His dream was to start a school to train rafting guides. He was good at it. Loved doing it. But every time he applied for licenses or tried to get a small business loan, he got turned down by the county."

"You think Brody was behind it?" If he was, that made what Reece had found even more menacing than he'd originally thought.

"I have no proof. It also could have been because of Noah's—" She held up a hand. "Because of any number of things."

There was more to the story, but Reece decided to let it go for now. He had bigger issues to deal with. Bigger bombshells to drop on her already battered life. "I have no idea what the story behind that partnership agreement is, but I do know something strange is going on with it."

"Why?" Paige glanced at the papers again, flipping through them, scanning as though she was finally actually reading the words.

He saw when she reached the very line that had also stopped him in his tracks.

The third partner in the venture between Brody Carson and Wild River Outdoors...was Noah Bristow.

* * *

Paige stared at the contract in her hand, her knees weak. This made no sense. Noah was working with...with Brody? Brody Carson, who'd been trying for years to shut down Howling Moon? "I don't understand."

Noah and Brody had tangled more than once over the refuge. Brody had cost them donors and sponsors through the years as he'd turned nearly half of the town against their animals and their mission. The man's ignorance about hybrids knew no bounds. When he'd seemingly blocked Noah's dreams of opening a rafting school, there had been even more tension between them.

More than once, Noah had paced the floor in the living room, his hands balled into fists, praying his way through. *It's so hard to forgive him, Paige. Even harder to pray for him. I don't know why he can't leave us alone.* It was in those moments of stress, especially near the end, when his hands had started to shake. Those small signs of his progressing disease had only served to agitate Noah more.

Yet he had signed a partnership deal with Brody? Without ever mentioning it to her? How was that possible?

"Mama?" Hailey's questioning voice came

from the other side of the room. "I'm hungry. Are we going to finish the eggs? I want to give some to Maverick."

Of course she did. Hailey's heart was with every animal that crossed her path. Like Paige and Noah both, she seemed to have been born with a soft spot for creatures who had no voice of their own.

Any questions about Noah would have to wait.

When Paige looked at Reece, he held out a hand to help steady her, but she ignored it. She was leaning on him too much, growing too comfortable with his presence and his protection.

His time here was limited, and this temporary blip of him in her life would end as soon as he was gone again. It had to.

"I'll help her. You sit at the table and see what you can figure out from that document." Reece whispered the words then laid his hand on the small of her back and guided her away from the counter. As soon as she stepped away, he raised his voice. "I hear you're a fabulous egg scrambler, Hailey. Want to teach me how?"

Paige stopped and looked up from the papers she'd been reading as she walked to the table. Wow. He was a natural with kids.

The thought brought guilt and nausea with

it. That kid he was teaching was his, and he didn't even know it.

She swallowed the pain. "How is it you know so much about children?"

Reece froze with his hand halfway to the dial on the stove. His shoulders tightened then relaxed. "I dated a woman a couple of years ago for a few months. She had a son a year or so younger than Hailey." The words were casual, and he turned the heat on under the skillet as though he hadn't gutted her with the story.

He'd had a girlfriend. One he'd dated seriously enough to get to know her child.

It was possible he had one now. Maybe he even had a fiancée. She had never thought to ask. Had assumed he'd never moved on from her.

How arrogant was that?

And how hypocritical?

Dropping into one of the chairs at the table, her back to the activity in the kitchen, she stared unseeing at the papers in her hand. Why should she be surprised? Reece was a caring, kind, handsome man. Any woman would jump at the chance to be loved by him.

Why should it matter to her? She'd walked away from him, not the other way around. She was the one hiding his child from him. He had every right to find someone else. To…to fall in love again.

Still, the thought of Reece with another woman nearly doubled her over.

She couldn't let him know. If she did, he'd learn the truth… He held a huge chunk of her heart.

A chunk that had left a hole bleeding out into her chest.

Behind her, Reece said something to Hailey and Hailey giggled her little-girl laugh.

The father-daughter time was killing her. Ripping her in two. She should have kept them apart. Should have sent Hailey to her room.

But she couldn't keep her daughter prisoner. And she couldn't lock Reece out of the house when she'd asked him to come here, even if it *had* been at Seb's urging.

Shoving away from the table, she walked outside with Luna at her heels and found a chair on the deck where she couldn't see into the kitchen or hear what was going on in there. Let Reece have time with the daughter he'd never know was his.

She held the contract in her shaking hands and tried to make sense of the words through the muddy mess in her brain. From what she could process through the gunk, Wild River Outdoors had agreed to open a river guide training center on the nearby Salmon River. Somehow, Brody and Noah were working together to bring the company to the area. If she was understanding correctly, Brody was fronting a large chunk of the money while Noah was providing the land.

Noah was providing the land? That made even less sense than the partnership itself. The only property Noah owned was where the refuge sat, and he only owned it free and clear because it had been passed down by his grandfather. Surely, he hadn't considered selling the refuge to Brody Carson. He'd have told Paige of a decision that monumental.

He hadn't even bothered to tell her he was going into business with Brody, so maybe he wouldn't have.

It still didn't add up. If Noah had plans to sell the refuge's land to Brody, then there would be no reason for him to continue his campaign to shut down Howling Moon.

She flipped to another page and found more details, including a land survey. While legal documents weren't her primary language, she could puzzle out enough to understand Noah wasn't selling any land. He was leasing a parcel to Brody and to Wild River.

It wasn't Howling Moon's land though. This land backed up to the refuge.

She lifted her eyes from the survey on the paper to the slope in front of her. Noah had always told her his land stopped at the top of the ridge, but it didn't. Another nine acres ran down the other side of the hill to the river.

Why wouldn't he tell her? They didn't need it for the refuge. Due to the steep rise at the top of the hill on the far side, it wasn't usable for them anyway. Fencing it would be impossible.

If Brody wanted the land, Noah could have sold it to him and put the money toward their struggling finances. While Brody could be arrogant and difficult to deal with, he was typically fair when it came to business. He would have paid a decent price for the acreage, she was certain.

Something must have gone wrong, if he was here yelling at Paige and throwing contract in her face.

Something that might explain the reasons Noah had lied.

TEN

If Brody Carson wanted an all-out war, then he was going to get it.

Reece killed his latest call and tapped his cell against his jeans-clad knee while he sat on Paige's couch. With every phone number he dialed and every web search he did, he grew more suspicious of Brody.

In the kitchen, Hailey sang some silly song about everybody cleaning up as she put away the dishes Paige washed. Occasionally, Paige joined in for a word or two, but she was largely silent, understandably distracted by the whirlwind of events in her life.

By the lie of omission her husband had committed.

Reece definitely knew betrayal. He could well imagine how Paige was feeling, especially when the person she needed answers from could never provide answers to her questions. She was likely angry and confused and questioning herself.

Yeah, he knew how that felt. While he'd forgiven her years ago, he was still surprised by the dull edge to his anger today. He'd expected to feel a lot more. Instead, he leaned more toward the confused...and the protective.

It was the kind of thing only God could do.

"Run and put on your boots." Paige's voice drifted over as the sounds from the kitchen changed.

Hailey stopped singing and bolted through the den, charging down the hall, Luna close behind. The wolf-dog was a fierce protector of mother and daughter alike. Last night, when Paige had finally let her out of the bedroom, Luna had bolted frantically around the house, yipping and howling. Whether she could smell Paige's attacker or could sense danger, there was no way of knowing.

Paige came over and sat on the opposite end of the couch, rubbing her hands together. The scent of lemon came with her, probably hand cream or dish soap. "Did you learn anything?"

"Yes and no." Normally he wouldn't be so candid with a victim, but this was Paige. He felt more partnership than he should. "I spoke to Brody's wife, the manager at his corporate office and the sheriff. I wouldn't be surprised if there's some blowback, because it's obvious I think he's a suspect."

"And?"

"Nobody knows where Brody was when Camelot was shot. Same for last night when you were assaulted." He continued tapping the phone against his knee, trying to fit the puzzle together. "He left the sheriff's office almost immediately after us, but I'm not sure that would have given him time to get back here to come at Daniel."

"It could if he sped and took the back way. We came up the main road and had to creep along Main Street. If Brody came up the other side of the mountain, he could have done it, but barely."

"What's the motive?" The brick wall was right there. Brody had no obvious reason to harm Daniel. "I can see Brody wanting to run you off if he really believes your animals are dangerous, and if they really did cost him a deal with Wild River, but things still don't add up."

"You talked to Wild River?" Paige had read the contract, more concerned with why Noah had kept silent about the land than about Brody's involvement.

Reece wanted to know what Brody was

blaming Paige for, because the motive could be in that story. "I did. They were all set to sign on the dotted line when Noah died, which stopped everything."

"Why not come to me? If it's Noah's land, then I own it now, right?" She gestured toward the mountain. "I'd gladly sell it to Brody. The money would keep this place running."

"I went to several offices in town." Here was the disheartening part. "There's a tax issue. Brody was likely hoping he could get it cheaper a different way."

"Maybe? But…how would I not know this? I open the mail. I should get a tax bill."

"Did Noah have an office?" If he was hiding something, that would be the first place to look.

She nodded to a door near the kitchen. "Down on the garage level. I haven't been in there since the accident. I grabbed a few things, but…" She shrugged. "It's possible I missed something."

"Mind if I take a look?" She might not want him digging through her husband's private affairs.

"Go ahead." She looked into the hall as Hailey raced back, wearing neon-pink rain boots and a bright green raincoat. Paige chuckled. "You planning for the bottom to fall out on you, kiddo? There's mud from last night, but it's not supposed to rain today."

"I like the color." With a flying leap, Hailey landed on the couch between them. "Let's go. I wanna see Hope and tell her Seb's taking care of Camelot." She turned suddenly and grabbed Paige's wrist. "Aunt Lacey said I get to come back and spend the night some more. We're going to cook out and make s'mores and have hot chocolate."

"They should be here around lunchtime. They went home to take a nap and get showers since they were up all night." She pressed a kiss to Hailey's forehead and stood. "Let's go finish feeding the animals."

Reece turned his attention from them to his email on his phone. Nothing new. He'd checked it five minutes earlier, but he couldn't watch. Every time they interacted, his heart tugged toward them.

That was the last thing he needed. He'd built a life in Denver *without* Paige. She'd built a life here *with* another man. Even though Noah was gone, it was clear she belonged at Howling Moon.

Besides, there was no way he could trust her with his heart again. It had taken over a year for it to start beating after she left.

When they walked out the door, Luna in tow,

he followed reluctantly. Even though he wanted to keep his distance, he couldn't let them out of his sight. Someone could be hiding in the shed or getting a bead on them through a rifle scope. He needed to stay vigilant.

Outside Hope's enclosure, Paige grabbed a bin and braced it on her hip. Reece hadn't noticed it before, but she'd probably dropped it when Brody had blown up at her. It was near where they'd been standing during the confrontation.

She commanded Luna to wait outside, eased open the enclosure door and then whistled two notes that brought Hope crashing out of the trees. The animal ran straight for the shelter when she saw Paige carrying the bin.

Feeding time.

As Hailey closed the gate, Reece leaned against the fence to watch. Maverick sat at his side, nose twitching.

Hailey hung back near Reece and absent-mindedly scratched Luna's ear while her mother fed Hope. "I don't get close when they eat. They might get mad."

"Smart girl." He looked down at Maverick. "Even this guy growls a little if you get between him and his food bowl."

"Maverick's too nice to growl, but I'll still be careful." He watched Paige check the area around the enclosure and document something on her phone. "I saw Camelot yesterday. Hope will be happy when he comes home. I'm sure she's lonely."

"Probably. With her companion gone, it's probably—" *Never mind.* He knew too well what that felt like. So much so that he almost considered camping in Hope's pen to keep her company.

As if she'd heard his thoughts, the wolf-shepherd bounded out of the small shelter like a spring under tension. She ran from one fence to the other then skidded to a stop in front of Paige. Paige stomped one foot on the ground, and Hope spun to run in the other direction, sliding on her front paws until she nearly hit the fence in front of Hailey. Crouching low, she looked up at the little girl, tail wagging.

Giggling, Hailey stepped away from Luna and moved to the right before skipping left.

Hope followed her every move.

In the perfect imitation of her mother, Hailey stomped one foot in front of Hope and the hybrid raced in a giant circle before tearing back toward Paige.

Reece couldn't help smiling. "Some game, huh?"

"Uh-huh. I taught her. She thinks it's fun."

Hailey laughed harder as Hope raced over and dropped in front of her for another round of play.

Even Luna jumped up to race along the fence line.

The kid was a natural with animals, like her mother. The way she'd known exactly how to approach Maverick, her cautious caring for Hope… She was smart, intuitive, compassionate, and everything he'd want in a kid someday.

Not that children were in his future. Not even a girlfriend to start climbing the family ladder with. The only woman he'd dated since Paige had cut out when he'd struggled with trust issues.

Reece was a confirmed bachelor with an apartment in Denver and a partner in Maverick. Outside of the job, he had nothing.

In the enclosure furthest from the house, near where the driveway exited the woods, two hybrids ran for the fence, jumping and tussling for position at the gate. The sound of a truck engine drew closer.

Luna stopped her pacing and trotted over to stand beside Hailey.

Reece tensed and turned away from the little family game. At least he had his gun and badge on him. He'd come across more official and less like a jealous ex.

Whoever it was, the animals weren't afraid. They seemed to be excited, jostling to be closest to whoever it was.

Seb's classic Chevy Blazer rounded the bend and emerged from the trees. Soon, every hybrid in every pen was at their gates, greeting the man who was clearly a favorite.

Either that or they had the same kind of appreciation for a classic truck that Reece did.

Seb pulled up next to Reece's SUV, shut off the engine and walked over to stand with him at Hope's gate. The man looked exhausted, but he nodded at Reece before he gave Luna a cursory pet then crouched to Hailey's eye level. "What's up, Hailey Bear?"

She threw her arms around Seb's neck and gave him a smacking kiss on the cheek. "Is it time to go make s'mores?"

Exiting the enclosure, Paige chuckled. "It's a little early for a campfire, kiddo."

"S'mores are for after sunset, when we light the firepit. I'm about to ride out to the Bishops' to check on their baby horse. Do you want to come along and see it?"

"Yes!" Hailey jumped up and down until Paige instructed her to run inside and grab her backpack.

As soon as she was gone, Paige turned to Seb. "Before Hailey gets back, I want to talk to you."

"About?"

"I want you to take Luna with you."

It almost looked like Seb flinched. He started to say something but then simply nodded. "I understand."

So did Reece. Paige was scared. Too scared to have her daughter or her beloved pet present on her own property.

Before he could comment, Paige's eyes narrowed and she studied Seb's face. "What's wrong?"

There she went again, with that uncanny ability to see past the surface. It was probably what made her a natural with the animals.

Seb dragged his hand down his face. "I got a call from Roaming Free on my way here."

Paige glanced at Reece. "They're a nonprofit out of Estes Park, and one of our biggest donors. I applied for an emergency grant." She turned to Seb, questions creasing her brow. "Why did they call you instead of me?"

He shrugged and looked at something beyond her near the large barn. "I don't know but... Paige?" When he finally looked at her, even Reece flinched at the blow that was obviously coming. "They turned down your grant application."

"What?" Paige was a flurry of motion, stalking to the Blazer and staring at the tire. "Why?"

"Someone called them and said the rescue isn't safe, that the animals have been getting hurt. So they denied the grant. And—"

"Stop." Paige crossed her arms and hung her head.

Seb didn't have to say it. Even Reece knew what was coming. The nonprofit had pulled its funding.

Bringing Paige even closer to ruin.

Pulling open the front door of Reece's SUV with enough force to rock him in his seat, Paige climbed into the vehicle and almost slammed the door shut again before she remembered Maverick. With a deep breath and a whole lot of restraint from somewhere higher than herself, she shut the door gently and stared out the windshield at downtown Crystal Ridge.

Tears threatened to explode from her throbbing throat. Her shoulder stung and her head throbbed, adding insult to those physical injuries and to the emotional pain she now endured.

The bank had refused to give her a loan without stable income, so she'd done the only thing she could do and dived into her options with Noah's secret property.

A quick visit to the county clerk's office had shredded the last of her hope. Within weeks, the refuge would shut down. She needed to start calling other rescues, trying to find homes for her animals. There was a hybrid sanctuary outside Denver that she'd worked closely with. They'd likely help.

Maybe she could call Austin Wyatt, offer him a chunk of the property adjoining his. She could keep a small parcel with the house and—

"Paige?" Reece interrupted her frantic planning. He hadn't started the truck. Instead, he simply watched her. "I take it things didn't go well?"

She'd been so busy trying to build her future that she hadn't even reported her findings to Reece. Sighing, she threaded the seat belt through her fingers, then let it snap into place, barely registering the sting. "Things went the opposite of *well*." The words were tight, forcing their way past tears she didn't want to shed. It felt as though all she'd done was cry in front of Reece.

"Want to talk about it?"

"Not really." Even as the words came out, she knew she needed to unburden herself. Reece was trustworthy and smart. He might be able to come up with something to keep the sanctuary afloat. *Please, Lord.*

She'd been praying for hours. So far, no answer had fallen from the sky. Not that she'd expected one, but it sure would have been nice.

She pivoted in the seat so she faced Reece. "Noah truly did own the land on the far side of the ridge. It's mine to sell.

"But he owes back taxes on the property. It's more money than I can dig up between the couch cushions. The land's only a couple of months away from being seized and going up for auction. Brody ought to be happy."

"Wait." Reece waved his hand between them as though he was trying to clear something rotten from the air. "How did you not know? You run Howling Moon. You see the mail. Something should have come since he died."

He'd hit upon the thing that cut the most. Leaning forward, Paige fished a folded paper from her hip pocket and passed it to Reece. Touching it made her feel somehow *less than*. "That's his cousin's address in Texas. Felicity is his only living relative. Although the property is Noah's and Noah's been the one paying the bill, the correspondence went to that address." Not to Howling Moon. It was proof that Noah had purposely kept the property hidden from her.

"So we call the cousin and—"

"She's deployed. It could take some time to reach her."

"By not notifying you, the town is skating very close to some legal issues here. I'm going to call an FBI contact and see if—"

"Reece, over half the town already hates me. I don't need to rain fire on everyone's heads by bringing in the FBI. If I do, then the run-Paige-out-of-town meter soars to one hundred percent." She deflated, wincing when her shoulder brushed the seat back. "Hailey starts kindergarten in a few weeks. She's already going to get flack for being the 'wolf girl.' I don't want to know what they'd say if her mother lit a scandal and upended the entire town government."

It looked like Reece was going to argue, but then he seemed to think better of it, pausing as though he could read his next sentence in the air. "Would Seb know about the property?"

"Maybe?" He'd been Noah's friend since childhood. "I want to ask him in person though, see his face." Seb had never lied to her before, but she'd always thought Noah had told her the truth about everything as well.

Suddenly, no one was safe.

Reece tapped the steering wheel with his thumb. "When I talked to Wild River, I asked why they backed out."

"And?"

"They heard about the town's movement against Howling Moon and became concerned about building an educational center next to a hybrid wolf rescue."

Oh, the irony. Brody's ignorance insistence on shutting her down had come back to bite him.

As for Noah's involvement, she could only guess. "Whatever reason Noah kept it from me, I'm thinking he planned to use the proceeds from the lease to keep the refuge afloat." It made sense. As his condition worsened, a steady income would have been invaluable.

Still, she couldn't imagine why he'd kept silent.

"You know, you could sell the land and pay off the tax lien with the proceeds. Profits would go into your pocket."

She'd been so blinded by her shock that she hadn't processed a way forward. Reece's information added a new dimension to her plans.

The balloon hit the ground as quickly as it rose. "Nobody will pay me top dollar when they find out about the auction. I can't stop the auction without paying the taxes. I can't pay the taxes without selling, and I can't sell without paying the taxes."

Oh, wouldn't this make Austin Wyatt salivate? If she sold Howling Moon to him and then he won the tax auction for the remaining land, he could own everything to the river.

Brody would be furious.

Reece reached started the SUV. "Well, here's our next move." Reece shifted into gear. "Wild River has a satellite office in Challis. We'll go there and see what they can tell us about the contract. As for the taxes, you should call your lawyer. You may have a case for postponing an auction."

"You think?" He buoyed her hopes once again, though not as high as before. It seemed like she kept climbing a mountain that grew taller with each step. Every day, running Howling Moon seemed to tax her more than fulfill her. Noah had always been the one to handle the business side of things while she worked with the animals. Trying to do both was dragging her lower with every hit that came.

"You're fully you at the refuge, the person you always wanted to be, working with the outcast animals. We'll find a way to keep you afloat." He pulled up to the parking lot exit and looked both ways. "I'd like to see you stay happy."

He said the words with such conviction that Paige wanted to grab his hand the way she used to when she'd belonged to him. When he'd believed she could do anything.

He'd been the only one to ever believe in her. Maybe he was right.

"Those animals have been rejected by their owners. Being with them makes me feel like I belong. Like I have value. Like I love them and they love me back with a pure love that will never go away." On days like today, when she thought of throwing in the towel and building a simpler life for herself and Hailey, the rescues kept her going.

Although sometimes she wondered if someone else couldn't take better care of them than she could.

Reece massaged the steering wheel as he made his way slowly up the main road. Several miles passed before he spoke. "I loved you like that." The words were low, husky with emotion.

The gut punch was real, but she couldn't do this. Not now. She was so spun about everything that she was likely to blurt the whole truth to him.

To do so would infuriate his mother and might even split his family. She couldn't wreck his life. Couldn't shatter what he believed about his family. They'd always been so important to him. It was one of the reasons she hadn't asked about them since he'd arrived. She couldn't risk dancing too close to a truth that could change Reece's existence forever.

Her inhale was shakier than she wanted it to be. "I know."

"Then why—"

"I just need you to accept my apology and trust I did the right thing."

"'The right thing'?" There was no anger. Instead, his tone was laced with questions and confusion. "What does that even mean?"

She'd said too much. It had been bound to happen and now she'd done it. All while stuck in a vehicle with nowhere to run. She was trapped. With Reece's questions and the past looming between them. With a truth she needed to keep secret to protect both him and Hailey.

"Don't ask—"

"Stop." Reece held a hand up between them, his eyes on the side mirror. His expression shifted to concern. "Something's wrong."

Paige's stomach clenched. She whipped around to look out the back of the SUV. The seat belt tweaked her shoulder but she turned farther, unable to see past Maverick's kennel.

The K-9 had stood and balanced on sure feet,

watching Reece. He seemed to be in tune with his handler's change in mood.

"Reece?" She slid lower in the seat and tried to see out her side mirror. All she could make out was a pickup truck in the distance, coming closer by the second. "Someone's following us?" She grabbed the door as Reece increased speed entering one of the mountain curves, a drop-off seeming to open up to her right. The road to Challis was winding and steep before it wended down to the town. This wasn't really the place to be putting on the gas.

"That truck came up fast. Too fast for conditions on this road, anyway." Reece gripped the steering wheel with both hands and snapped a command to Maverick, who laid down, although his head remained upright, his ears raised.

Yeah, he could sense something was up.

Paige watched the truck as it loomed larger in the mirror. If he didn't slow down, he was going to—

The impact knocked her forward against the seat belt. Tires squealed. Maverick barked.

Reece's SUV skidded toward the cliff.

ELEVEN

Drawing on every moment he'd spent in defensive driver's training, Reece let off the gas and turned the wheel into the skid.

The SUV rocked as it fought his efforts to straighten it, then came back into control as he entered the curve. *What is this guy doing?*

He didn't ask the question aloud. He already knew.

Whoever was behind the wheel of the huge blue pickup was trying to kill Paige, and he didn't care who he took out with her. Even if he murdered a law enforcement officer.

"This is escalating." He muttered the words, knowing they were obvious but needing to vent them.

Paige didn't seem to hear. If she did, she kept her response to herself. It was possible she was praying, same as he was, though his prayers were more screaming emotions than coherent thoughts as the engine roared louder.

The road straightened slightly, and the truck backed off. Distance allowed Reece to grab a quick breath and assess. The way the light hit the windshield of the truck, it was impossible to see anything other than the vague shape of the driver. No help there.

He glanced at the GPS on his dash. They were only a couple of miles from the foot of the mountain, where the road would level out and this guy wouldn't be as much of a threat.

It would be a long couple of miles of steep descent on narrow roads. *Lord, I could use a hand here.* He prayed the only prayer he could think of, quick and to the point, but he had no doubt he'd been heard.

Now he had to hang on and trust his training. "If we go over the side, get out as soon as you can and run. Don't wait for me or Maverick." It was a false plan meant to keep Paige calm, every word of it. If they went over the side, with the steepness of the cliff, they'd likely plummet to their deaths. Still, he needed to give Paige something to focus on. Maybe even needed to give himself a bit of false hope.

"Yeah, right." Her murmur probably wasn't meant to be spoken aloud. She didn't believe him, and he really wasn't surprised. Instead, she held on tighter to the door, her lips moving slightly. No doubt she was praying as hard as he was.

Reece tightened his hold on the steering wheel. As they headed into another curve, the pickup's engine roared behind them as the truck blasted forward for another assault on Reece's rear bumper, trying to induce a spin.

The guy had watched too much television. PIT maneuvers had to be precise or both vehicles would end up in trouble. If this guy kept speeding on this road the way he was, they might both wind up over the side before there was another impact. "Hang on."

Praying there wasn't a car coming from the opposite direction, Reece edged closer to the center line, absorbing the next hit in a central location on the bumper. The force shoved them forward, not sideways, and he was able to maintain control going into the turn.

That wouldn't last long. His only hope was to somehow maneuver so his pursuer became the pursued. He had to get behind the truck.

At the next straight section of road, Reece gunned the engine and raced forward, the pickup keeping pace behind him at a couple of car lengths distance, likely waiting for the next turn.

If the truck got another shot, it would likely be the kill shot.

Unless...

"Hold on." He had one idea and it had better work. His heart hammered and his palms were slick on the steering wheel. He usually didn't sweat dangerous situations, but Paige was involved in this one. If he lost her again...

He'd never known any thought more terrifying.

With no cars coming toward him, Reece uttered one more prayer. *Lord, let this work.*

He took a bracing breath, practically slammed on the brakes and jerked the SUV into the opposite lane. The whole vehicle rocked and lurched, throwing them forward against the seat belts.

Paige gasped.

The pickup blew past, tires screeching as the driver slammed on his brakes and nearly went sideways into the upcoming turn before he righted himself, gunning the engine to speed away.

Reece didn't waste any time watching to see the outcome. Flooring the gas, he spun the tires as he swerved into the correct lane in pursuit.

"Stop." Paige grabbed his shoulder, her fingers digging in, panic-laced trembles almost overriding her ability to speak. "You'll never make the next turn at this speed. It's a hairpin." She shoved her finger against the GPS screen.

Sure enough, the road ahead doubled back on itself. Survival instinct overrode the adrenaline of pursuit. Reece slowed but continued on. "I'm not letting him get away."

"You don't have to follow him. I got a good look at the truck when it passed. I know who it belongs to."

Reece lifted his foot off of the accelerator and allowed the SUV to coast to a safer speed, glancing in the mirror to make sure no one was coming up on them. "Was it Brody's?" When he glanced at Paige, her mouth was a tight line, her face devoid of color. He'd never seen lips so pale.

"No." She pulled her hand from his shoulder and clasped her fingers between her knees. "The license plate was a vanity plate with *FW* at the start. It's from the Flying W Ranch, Austin Wyatt's place on the other side of the logging road from me."

"The guy who keeps asking to buy your land?" She'd mentioned him briefly but, while he was on Reece's list of suspects, he wasn't as high as Brody Carson.

Well, he'd definitely earned a spot at the top of the list.

"Tell me the fastest route to get there." Reece

rounded the curve and found a side road to make a turn. "Unless that driver spins around and overtakes us, we'll beat whoever it is to the ranch. There's not a back way, is there?" He reversed onto the road and headed in the direction of Crystal Ridge and the refuge.

"There is, but it tacks on a half hour to the drive. You're taking the shortest route. Unless he comes back and passes us, we'll get there first."

They drove in silence for several minutes. Reece alternated between watching the road in front of him and keeping an eye on the road behind him. If this was a normal situation, he'd have called local law enforcement for backup, but not knowing who was in league with whom, a call for help could land them in deeper trouble.

The pickup didn't make a return appearance, and Reece breathed easier as they rolled slowly through downtown Crystal Ridge. As much as he wanted to gun it, to make absolutely certain he beat this Austin Wyatt guy back, he couldn't risk speeding through a pedestrian-filled tourist town. "I'm going straight to the ranch. We can go to Challis later and talk with Wild River."

Paige ran her hands through her hair and tucked it behind her ear. Her fingers shook, likely from the fear and adrenaline of yet another violent act, this one clearly meant to end both of their lives.

"I don't want to think about what I might find." She stared out the side window. "It could be Noah was—" Her words dropped suddenly, and she leaned forward in the seat. "Reece." Her head tilted toward something out the front window.

He followed her gaze. Two men stood in front of the county clerk's office, watching them with unconcealed interest.

Brody smiled as they passed, while the sheriff tipped his hat before they both turned and entered the building.

If she wasn't certain of Reece's goal to catch Austin red-handed rolling back into the ranch, Paige would demand he stop the truck. She'd jump out and cause a scene right in the middle of Crystal Ridge in front of tourist and towns-folk alike. It didn't matter who was looking or what they thought.

All of the fear and adrenaline and anger bubbled up inside her, a capped geyser ready to blow. She couldn't take the veiled threats any longer.

Who's trying to kill me? Why won't you do something? The accusations begged to fly in the sheriff's face, but she bit them back. Given how easily Brody's fearmongering had turned town sentiment against the refuge, Paige screaming in the sheriff's face in public during the height of tourist season would only solidify the town's resentment toward her. In their eyes, her precious animals were already a danger in their own backyards. They'd immediately label Paige as a danger as well. *Violent. Unstable. Angry.*

Not only would the refuge fail to survive such notoriety, an incident like that would ruin Hailey's chance to have a happy, healthy kindergarten experience…if she even had a chance to begin with.

"Well, that was interesting. Think they're trying to make sure you don't put a halt to the tax proceedings?" Reece's voice was level, but it was tight with tension. Like her, he was probably torn in too many directions.

There was no way he wasn't at least a little shaken by the events of the past half hour. Any human being would be.

She knew she could use a strong cup of coffee and maybe a few years of therapy over the incident. Her supply of false bravado was quickly running short.

"Paige?" Reece cut through her thoughts. "You okay?"

"Oh, I'm amazing. Absolutely peachy keen." Before he could speak, she plowed ahead. "I'm doing the best I can. I'm glad Hailey is with Seb and Lacey." The last thing she needed was sympathy or pity, especially when all she wanted was for him to pull over and let her rest her head against his chest again. In his arms, she felt safe.

Reece shook his head, his jaw tight as he slowed at the entrance to the Flying W Ranch, but he kept quiet about her sarcasm.

Instead, he eyed the property. A split-rail fence ran along the front of the ranch, and an arched entry gate held a swinging sign: Flying W Ranch. "Tell me about this guy."

"Not much to tell. He's always been cordial if a little standoffish. He's not a part of the whole *run those violent wolves out of town* contingent. The few times he's been to the ranch, he's been friendly to the animals. Still, he's constantly talking about how much he'd like to buy the land. Since before Noah died, he's been wanting to expand his operation, but he's land-locked by our property. He used to hit Noah up about once a month about selling, but since... Well, since the accident, he's been reaching out weekly. I'm pretty sure he knows the refuge is having money issues. Thing is, he's never once offered me a price that would allow me to up and move this place. It's more than he could ever come up with, I'm sure."

"So he lowballs the offer?"

"Not exactly. It would take a small fortune to pack up my animals and build an entirely new habitat somewhere else. What we have would be hard to duplicate without a huge outlay for land, permits and structures. Not to mention, I'd have to have a place for Hailey and me to live. It's one of the reasons I stay despite the hatred Brody has stirred up. This is the only home Hailey has ever known." The foundation of that home was growing more unstable every day.

"I can imagine."

As they wended their way along fenced pastureland, a large white ranch house came into view. Paige had to admit it was an impressive sight. Austin Wyatt clearly lived his life like he was every inch the big-time cattle rancher he dreamed of being. He and his wife, Callie, were second only to the Carsons when it came to money and status in Crystal Ridge. It always seemed to bite at them that they came in second. There was no love lost between the Wyatts and the Carsons.

There was also no love lost between Paige and Austin at the moment. Someone connected to the ranch—possibly Austin him-self—had tried to kill her. She balled her fists, ready to unleash her pent-up emotions on him. There was nothing to hold her back. The town couldn't see her tirade out here.

As they approached the house, Reece arched an eyebrow and tipped his head at something out the windshield. "Interesting."

Paige followed his gaze, recognizing the SUV parked in front of the house. "That's a county vehicle."

Sure enough, as they glided to a stop behind the law enforcement vehicle, Austin and a dep-uty she recognized as Mariah Haleema looked up from a conversation at the top of the porch steps. Austin's wife sat on a nearby rocking chair, but she stood and moved to stand beside Austin as Reece's SUV approached.

"Looks like Austin has an alibi." Reece shut off the engine. He commanded Maverick to stay in the vehicle, then stepped out. He was at Paige's door before she could slide out of the vehicle. "I know you want to demand answers and maybe even get up in his face, but I need you to stand down and let me do the talking."

Paige dug her fingernails into her palms. Reece had always been able to tell when she was about to burn to the end of her short fuse.

Right now, the flame was definitely about to hit black powder. She wanted to shove past him and loose her anger and fear on Austin.

Wisdom and the Jesus in her said Reece was right. She needed to keep this professional and let him do the talking.

Maybe she ought to stay in the SUV with Maverick.

If she did, she might crawl right out of her skin wondering what was happening. She needed to hear firsthand what Austin Wyatt had to say. "Okay."

Reece reached for her hand, gently unfolded her clenched fingers then laced them briefly with his own. "Trust me." He squeezed and let go.

She did. More than she probably should.

"Afternoon." Reece mounted the steps with Paige just behind him and addressed Deputy Haleema first. "Officer Reece Campbell, Rocky Mountain K-9 Unit."

"Officer." She nodded to Reece, her short dark ponytail swinging forward slightly.

Paige fought hard to ignore the green pang swimming through her stomach. Mariah attended the same church as her family and was a by-the-book law enforcement officer, patient and fair, but tough. She was also one of the most beautiful women Paige had ever laid eyes on. Watching her introduce herself to Reece unnerved her almost as much as being run off the road.

That shouldn't be. There was no personal interaction between the two officers. It was clearly all business. Even if one of them had showed evidence of noticing the other in a different way, it was none of her business.

Oh, how she wanted it to be her business.

Mariah glanced at her with a curious look. "Good afternoon, Paige."

Paige nodded a hello and focused on Reece, who wasted no time diving into his questions.

"Mr. Wyatt, have you been home all afternoon?"

Furrowing his brow, Austin dipped his chin, clearly suspicious and on guard with this newcomer. "Mind if I ask what I'm being accused of?"

"About half an hour ago, someone driving a pickup bearing one of your ranch's license plates attempted to force my vehicle off the road."

Callie gasped and reached for Austin's elbow.

Paige sank her teeth into her lip. Reece had left her out of the equation, but there was likely a good reason for it. She'd wait to see where he led the conversation.

With a glance at Paige, Austin turned his attention to Reece. "That's why Deputy Haleema's here. At some point after about five last night, somebody stole the plate off one of my work trucks out in the barn."

"Convenient." The word spilled from Paige's mouth before she could stop it.

Reece shot her a hard look as Callie straightened and fired off a stare that should have melted Paige right on the spot. "Do you have something to say, Paige?"

"Ladies." Deputy Haleema stepped closer to their small circle then faced Reece. "Mr. Wyatt has a work truck in the back barn that's been out of commission for several weeks. He was working on it yesterday afternoon and everything was fine. When he went out after lunch today to continue, he noticed the plate was missing. I arrived about half an hour ago and we've been out to the barn to investigate already."

"Who has access to the barn?" Reece addressed the deputy.

"All of the ranch hands, but they're all accounted for."

Austin pointed to the right, toward an open pasture. "They've been working cattle today. We're rounding up for a head count so I can finalize planning for fall sales." He pulled his arm from Callie's grasp to scratch beneath his tan Stetson. "They're all on the other side of the ranch, but I called over to my foreman and he's got everyone accounted for."

If Austin had been there for over half an hour and all of the hands were on site, then someone off the ranch had come after them. Nobody on the porch could have done it. They'd all been with the deputy.

Yeah, it did sound awfully convenient. It wouldn't have been hard to have an accomplice take the truck and make a run at them.

Austin turned to Paige. "Were you with the officer when this happened?"

She nodded.

Callie stepped forward, the earlier anger dropping from her expression. "Are you okay? Hailey wasn't with you, was she?"

"No." Once again, waves of nausea crested. If her daughter had been injured... No. That was a mental road she didn't want to travel. She looked at her feet. "Hailey is safe with friends."

Callie's frown deepened. "I'm sorry that happened to you, but the way Brody's got sentiment in this town turned against you, it doesn't surprise me someone's gotten worked up enough to go this far. That man needs to—"

"Callie." Austin slipped an arm around his wife's waist. "Now's not the time." He pulled her closer as he addressed the two law enforcement officers. "I've got cameras in various places on the property. I'll see if they picked anything up."

"I'll get a warrant for those. Make sure everything is aboveboard if you do find something." Reece's voice was hard. He backed down a step but Paige hesitated.

What was Reece doing, leaving without asking more questions? Surely he didn't believe the story about the license plate. It was too easy.

He tugged lightly on the back of her shirt as he descended another step.

She didn't want to leave. They were close to answers but, without Reece's badge to back her up, there was nothing more she could do.

She followed him, but he stopped halfway to the truck and turned to pin Austin with a hard, unreadable gaze. "I will say this, Mr. Wyatt. I know you have a vested interest in Mrs. Bristow leaving Crystal Ridge. That gives you motive. I'd suggest that, until we find out who's behind this, you keep your distance."

TWELVE

Curling onto her side on her bed, Paige stared at the window where the open curtains allowed a view of orange and red sunset clouds streaking the sky. The light in the room was tinted in those same hues. It was probably gorgeous with the colors streaming over the mountain, but she couldn't bring herself to care. Couldn't muster enough energy to get off the bed and see the sight for herself.

She'd taken a shower, desperate to relieve tight muscles, and hoping to wash fear down the drain.

It hadn't worked.

After tugging on shorts and an old sweatshirt, she'd made it as far as her bed before her shaking limbs decided they'd go no further.

God, I can't do this anymore. It had all spun too far out of control. Her mind couldn't stop playing images of Reece's SUV flying off the mountain. Of what might have happened if she'd been driving her pickup and Hailey had been in the back seat.

The next time a hit came, she'd likely be alone with Hailey.

Reece couldn't stay here forever playing bodyguard to her. If they didn't find out who was behind the attacks on her life and on her rescues soon, he'd have to go back to his team and leave her here alone. As soon as he was gone, she had no doubt whoever was out to get her would escalate once again.

Was it Brody? Austin? A disgruntled townsperson riled up by Brody's constant campaign of misinformation against Howling Moon?

Lord, show us. Show us what we're missing. And show me if it's time to give up on this dream.

Her biggest donors were gone. Even if she could sell the extra land, did she want to? It would only be a bandage to cover a wound that grew more infected every time a bill rolled in.

The thought of quitting gutted her. She loved every animal at Howling Moon.

But did she love them enough to let them go?

Seriously, God. What do we do?

What she wanted was a handwriting-on-the-wall kind of thing, like in the Bible. A clear answer. Something they couldn't miss.

What she got was silence broken only by the low hum of Reece's voice as he chatted with someone on the phone in the living room.

She tucked her hands between her knees and curled into a tighter ball as though she could somehow block his presence from her heart.

It didn't work. He'd found his way there anyway. When she'd left six years ago, she'd walled up the room where the love she'd felt for him lived. Over the years, her feelings had stopped kicking at those emotional bricks until she'd assumed they were dead. Gone. After all, she'd married Noah and, although their marriage had been unconventional, she'd loved him faithfully and had truly been prepared to walk beside him through the coming hard times in his life, all the way until the *till death do us part* of their union. He'd been her cheerleader and closest confidant. Her protector and partner. She missed his presence in the house. His constancy in her life. His care and love for Hailey, as though she truly was his own.

With Noah gone and Reece back, she had to face facts. Her love for Reece had been dormant, quiet. Starving for the nourishment it had finally received when he'd walked back into her life.

Love had sprung back up with a vengeance, kicking down the walls until she had to admit the truth. He still held her heart. Only this time, it was different. This time, the butterflies and the wild, desperate need to be loved and to belong to somebody were gone. This time, her feelings for him were solid and steady; traits she'd learned from sacrificially loving Noah and accepting his sacrificial love in return. Traits she'd learned after Noah had introduced her to Jesus.

Yes, she longed for Reece because she felt safe whenever he was nearby and, most of all, when he held her. But there was something about him that fit and made her feel truly whole, as though he were the missing puzzle piece in her life. There was an extra *click* with Reece. One that finally made her feel like she was where she belonged.

There was no indication his feelings for her had survived, not past the pain she occasionally saw flicker in his expression. And not past the handful of times he'd asked her the hard questions she could never answer.

She turned her face into the pillow. That was the problem. What she felt didn't matter. What *he* felt didn't matter. He could walk in right now and drop to one knee, professing his eternal love and devotion. It wouldn't change a thing.

His mother would destroy her. His family would never accept her. She'd have to face his brother, who had repeatedly demanded things she would never give him.

A soft tap on the door jerked her upright. How had Reece made it up the hall without her hearing his footsteps? She cleared her throat and dragged her hands down her face. Good thing she hadn't given in to the tears she'd been holding back for what felt like years. "Yeah?"

"Can you come downstairs?" His voice was muffled by the closed door. "I need to talk to you about some things."

Her heart hammered a couple of extra beats. *Some things* could be anything from the threats against her life to why she'd disappeared on him so many years ago.

Or he could have come to the realization that Hailey shared an awful lot of likenesses with him.

She didn't want to talk about any of that, but she ran her hands through her damp hair and finger-combed a few knots. "I'll be out in a minute."

This time, she clearly heard his retreat down

the hall. It took all she had left to get herself out the door and into the living room, where Reece stood at the large picture window, staring out at the mountain.

He glanced over his shoulder when she walked in. "Sky's pretty."

Paige sank to the edge of Noah's old gray recliner and ran her hands down her thighs. "I saw it upstairs." *Sort of.* She'd love to see it, but crossing the room to admire the sunset with him was the last thing she needed to do. "What's up?"

Without turning from the window, he said, "I spoke to a friend of mine at the Iowa State Police. They found a blue pickup, with Austin Wyatt's stolen plate, abandoned on the outskirts of Challis."

Her head jerked up. "Whose truck is it?"

"Stolen. Somebody snatched it from a hotel in Crystal Ridge when a tourist left it unattended to run inside and get his bags. We're working on getting a warrant for those cameras and for Austin's as well."

Paige sat back in the chair, deflated and defeated. Every time they got close, someone slammed the door in their faces. "Now what?"

"We keep digging." He came over and sat on the coffee table, facing her. His knees were inches from hers. "We can't deny all of this is coordinated. Someone seemingly stole a plate from one of the Flying W vehicles, though I have no idea why. Can you think of any reason someone would want to make it look like Austin Wyatt wants you dead?"

"No." She threw her hands up and tried to think of any connection between them that could lead to deadly motives. There was nothing.

Reece puffed out a breath and stared at the floor between them. "Well, I have one solid lead. Whoever it was knew where to wait for an easy score. They knew where to wait for us. The question is who? Did you talk to Seb about any of this yet?"

"No." In the wake of everything else, the land had dropped to a low priority. Paige gripped her knees. What she really wanted to do was to reach for Reece's hands and hold on tight. "I don't understand my life anymore." Not who was coming after her, and certainly not about him. She needed him to leave before his mother descended and destroyed Hailey's world. But she also needed him to stay to hold on to any sense of safety. "How's your family?"

She sucked air in through her teeth. *No way. No.* Even from a distance, his mother was messing with her mind. She had never meant to ask about them. Had never intended to even hint about them. That question was playing with a lighted match next to an open gas barrel. Paige slammed her mouth shut.

Reece's head jerked back and he looked to the side as though he was watching the change in conversation fly past. "I… Well…" He looked at her briefly then stared at something over her shoulder near the front door. "Mom and Dad are divorced. She's living her never-get-off-the-treadmill attorney life. He retired early and did the cliché thing where he bought a boat and a lake cabin. I guess he needed more quiet than she did."

"I'm sorry." Reece's dad had always been cordial, but not overly friendly, at least not when Tabitha was around. She opened her mouth to ask about his brother then closed it again. If she danced too close to the flame, her entire life might go up in smoke.

As the silence stretched, Reece met her eye and seemed to read her expression. She couldn't look away, although she really wanted to.

"You didn't ask about Quentin."

Paige shrugged and stood, walking into the kitchen. Her voice refused to cooperate. She filled a glass with water and drained it, trying to ignore the way her hand shook. Hearing his name brought back the what-might-havebeens of the night he and his friends had tried to shove their way into her apartment. Of the next day when he'd been so smug as his mother had ruthlessly sliced her future to ribbons.

"Paige." Reece's voice dropped. It held an uncharacteristic hesitation. He walked over and stood on the other side of the island, his fingers pressing into the Formica counter. "I need you to be honest with me about something."

Her shoulders stiffened. He knew. Somehow, he knew. Her head shook back and forth. *No.* She wouldn't tell him. It was too shameful. He'd think she'd brought it on to herself. He'd—

"Quentin's in jail."

Paige's jaw slacked. She reached for the counter behind her and settled the glass carefully, trying not to let him see the tremor in her hand. "He is?" The words squeaked out, hoarse and uneven.

"I won't go into why." This time, the pain in his voice wasn't caused by something she'd done. "I've always wondered if he..." Reece cleared his throat. "If he ever said or did something when I wasn't around."

How long had he carried that awful question? She'd not been around for him to answer it because she'd let Quentin and his mother intimidate her. Let Tabitha buy her silence...

Buy her silence. Hailey's money. Tabitha could still take Hailey's future away, but that didn't mean Paige had to be selfish. She'd not asked Reece a single thing about his life since he'd arrived. She'd been so wrapped up in her fear of his mother finding out that she'd ignored Reece's feelings.

She went to him. Rounded the island before she even realized it. Wrapped her arms around his waist and rested her cheek against his beating heart.

Only this time she wasn't asking him to hold her up. Wasn't taking anything away.

She wanted to give him what she'd taken from him for too many years.

Even if it cost her everything.

What havoc had his brother wrought in Paige's life?

Reece wrapped his arms around her and held her close, the way he should have done years ago. Was this why she'd run? Had Quentin done something? Said something? Nothing else could explain her trembling or her sudden change in demeanor.

Quentin had hurt her. Rage and fear heated his skin and soured his stomach. *Please God, no.*

"Paige, I need to know." In Quentin's senior

year of college, his crimes had caught up to him when several women spoke up with stories even his mother couldn't bury. She hadn't been able to rescue him from the horror of his actions or to buy him out of his sentence either.

"This isn't about me right now." Paige's words vibrated against his chest. "This is about you. I can't…" She tightened her arms around his waist. "I can imagine what Quentin did, but I can't imagine how you must feel."

Something in Reece collapsed onto itself. Tension he hadn't realized he'd been carrying in his shoulders and his spine seemed to melt with Paige's acceptance and in her embrace.

No one had ever cared how he felt. His father had turned reclusive at the news. His mother had fought and clawed and screamed her way through the investigation and the trial, all of her attention focused on the son she could not believe was guilty of the crimes multiple women had accused him of.

While Reece had been a grown man, he'd still longed to have someone to pour himself out to. He'd sought a therapist at one point before joining the Denver PD. He'd found healing in helping others, and he'd learned to cope, but he'd never received the kind of acceptance he felt in this moment with Paige.

"I can't seem to forgive him." They were words he didn't like to admit to himself even in the silence of dark nights when he lay awake wondering why. Quentin had always been arrogant and a little hard to get along with, but...

In a million years, Reece never would have imagined him capable of causing so much pain. "I think I have and then... Then I get angry all over again." Like now, at the thought of his brother laying even one finger on Paige.

His emotions were especially high when he was assigned to cases involving women who'd been harmed. Those were the ones he threw himself into the most, seeking justice and maybe atonement for missing the truth for so many years.

"The thing I've learned?" Paige slipped her arms from around him and looked into his face. "Forgiveness is a choice. One we sometimes have to make moment to moment. In a situation like that?" She glanced away, then looked back at him with the slightest sheen of tears in her eyes. "When the pain was inflicted on someone innocent? Well... Those might be the hardest to forgive."

She was right, but he couldn't consider her words until he knew the answer to the question she'd dodged earlier. "Did he do anything to you?" He'd lain awake nights shoving the thought to the side, never fully addressing it. Burying it on the drive from Denver, so he wouldn't think of it every time he looked at her. It would destroy him to know Quentin had hurt Paige.

He couldn't deny he needed to know.

"He never laid a hand on me." The words were quick and frank, harboring no emotion.

Reece's muscles almost dropped him. He hadn't thought it possible to feel such relief.

Something in his heart let go. Some undefined fear he hadn't realized had frozen his blood and kept him mired in the past. "I'm sorry."

"For what?" She walked to the refrigerator then brought back a bottle of water. "You aren't responsible for his actions. You have to let the guilt go."

Reece took a sip of the icy water, letting the cold run down his throat to soothe some of the burn in his soul. "You sound like my therapist after the trial." Quentin had refused a plea deal. The trial had been brutal and the sentencing as tough as the law would allow. "I'm surprised you didn't know. It made the news."

"I'm selective about the news." She waved a hand toward the den. "Noah didn't own a TV. I get quick news and weather off the internet."

So she'd never checked to see how he was

doing. That stung. He'd lost count of the number of times he'd had to stop himself from googling her after her wedding.

That was the key, wasn't it? She'd married someone else. She'd had no reason to search for him.

For the millionth time, he wondered why she'd married someone else so quickly. If Noah had been in the background all along.

He knew Paige too well to believe that. "Paige? I—" His phone vibrated. Everything inside him rebelled at the intrusion, but he closed his eyes and shifted his focus. The call was probably interrupting what might be an ill-advised question. There wasn't an answer that would make the pain go away.

He pulled away reluctantly and glanced at the phone. Jodie Chen, Tyson's assistant. Maybe she'd finished the background checks on Daniel, the sheriff and Brody. He'd shot her a text earlier and added Austin Wyatt as well.

Paige squeezed his hand and walked away to straighten the kitchen.

Letting her go was getting harder, but it was for the best. He had work to do.

Reece answered the call. "Jodie. You have some intel for me?"

"You assume I'm calling about work and not

to see how your mental health is while you're protecting your ex."

"Your sarcasm is duly noted." He walked to the window in the den and looked out at the enclosures. It was nearly dark, and the animals were close to their shelters. Daniel must have come by to feed them. Paige had said he was anxious to return. "I figured you were calling about those background checks."

"I have a few things, but I have two Austin Wyatts in Lemhi County. Wanted to verify which was yours."

They ran through several bits of info, enough for Jodie to pinpoint their specific suspect.

Jodie muttered under her breath as her keystrokes clicked over the line. "I've found some interesting stuff on the others, but I want to make sure Austin Wyatt doesn't offer any detours. Can you talk in half an hour?"

"I can be."

From the kitchen, Paige glanced over at him, probably alerted by the veiled tone in his voice. She was perceptive enough to know the conversation had shifted into her direction.

Reece turned to the window. He needed a minute to remind himself he had a life in. This would never work.

Switching gears might let his head get back

into the game. He needed to talk about something less volatile than her case, just long enough to give his heart and his brain a break. "How's Shiloh doing?" The new K-9 recruit was a favorite of Jodie's and had been involved in the overheating incident in the kennels.

"He's a lot better today. Was pretty lethargic in the wake of the incident." Something in Jodie's voice carried the heat of a sheepish blush.

Reece sat on the edge of the recliner, taking a moment away from the wild storm in his emotions to focus on someone else. "What are you not saying?"

"I may or may not have slept at the kennel last night to make sure he was okay."

Reece chuckled. He knew that feeling, when one of the trainees wormed their way into your heart. Reaching down, he scratched Maverick behind the ears.

He should caution her against becoming too attached to a trainee, but it would probably be in vain. Besides, Jodie had worked with K-9s long enough to know the dangers. "I'm glad he's okay."

"Same. Oh, and here's something else you'll be interested in." Jodie's voice shifted to all-business. "There's news about Kate Montgomery."

The unit had been wrapped up in the Montgomery case, some regularly praying for the woman who'd nearly died in a staged car accident and had spent months in a coma until recently. Her friend Nikki Baker's baby had been kidnapped in the incident, and Nikki had been found dead shortly after, leaving more questions than answers about why someone had taken baby Chloe, killed Nikki and attempted to kill Kate.

"Is she okay?" She'd been touch and go before finally awakening and moving into rehab. They all had concerns about her health, both physically from the trauma and mentally from the emotional toll.

"She's doing fabulously at rehab, even remembering small details of the days leading up to the wreck, but nothing specifically about Nikki or her baby, and nothing about the incident itself."

"Any progress otherwise?"

"They've brought in a local therapist, Bryan Gold. He's a rock star at helping patients recover memories. We could start getting answers soon. We might even find the baby."

Please, Lord. He'd prayed so often for little Chloe Baker. There was evidence traffickers might have been involved, but there were also questions about Nikki's connections to the Maddox crime family.

Kate Montgomery's case had as many twists as Paige's did.

And that was the case he should be focusing on. He finally felt like he'd disengaged his emotions and could come at the clues with a new sense of clarity. He also needed to take a look at Noah's office. That would offer the privacy he needed to talk to Jodie, along with the opportunity to see if there was anything in Noah's personal affairs that merited further investigation. "So, half an hour?"

"Definitely."

"Give me a call. I'll be available." Because focusing on the threat against Paige was the only way to keep his head on straight and his heart out of the equation.

THIRTEEN

Midnight had come and gone as Reece and Paige discussed Quentin's trial and his sentencing. For the first time, someone had let Reece do the talking. He'd been able to unburden himself the way he never had before.

To Paige, of all people. The woman he'd loved and lost and... Yeah, he couldn't consider her found again. There was too much yet to be discussed.

Too keyed up to sleep, he'd finally stepped away from Paige to search Noah's office.

At the foot of the stairs that led from the living area to the garage, Reece stopped and let the darkness envelop him, taking a break from Paige's presence. Upstairs held that vague scent of her shampoo and something he had always associated with her. It blended a sense of past joy and current confusion.

Now he could go into investigative mode and leave the emotions with her.

He patted Maverick's head where the K-9 stood beside him. "We've got this, partner. You aren't planning to run off on me, are you?"

He rolled his eyes. Had he really said that? It had been six years, but he couldn't deny the longer he was with Paige, the more their past swamped him.

"Come on, Mav. Let's solve this mess and get out." Except something in him didn't want to. The equilibrium of his world had rocked. Would he be able to go back to Denver and act as though he'd detoxed Paige from his system when he clearly hadn't?

Man, he was a scattered mess when he needed to focus.

He flipped the light switch and illuminated the large garage. The wall beside him held a workbench and various tools organized on pegs. Paige's extended-cab pickup sat in the center of the floor. What had originally been the second garage bay had been walled off and converted into Noah's office.

Paige had told him she'd grabbed what she'd needed after Noah died and had never returned. She preferred to use the kitchen table and the guest room because they had natural light and she wasn't far from Hailey when working.

At the door, Reece hesitated. It gave him pause to go through Noah's things, like he was digging up dirt on Paige's husband.

What if he found something that implicated Noah in illegal activity? There was no indication of wrongdoing, but the most unlikely people hid the darkest secrets. If Noah was one of those people…then what?

He stretched tight neck muscles. Well, then, he'd do his job.

Shoving doubts aside, Reece pushed the door open. This was like any other search on any other investigation.

Beside him, Maverick waited for a command. On duty all of the time, the K-9 was unable to understand this wasn't the typical crime scene search for blood or trace evidence.

"Search." Reece set Maverick into motion to keep him busy. Early on, Reece had lost several pairs of shoes and a favorite windbreaker to a bored Maverick.

As expected, Maverick returned and sat at Reece's side, his huge tongue hanging out as he panted in expectation of a reward.

"Good job, partner." Reece pulled a treat from

his leg pocket and offered it to the K-9, who practically inhaled it. "Relax."

Maverick lay down and watched Reece to see what would come next.

Stepping over his partner, Reece surveyed the room. Painted plywood was covered with photos of wolves. Two filing cabinets sat against one wall and a desk was pushed against another. Noah's diploma and a few certificates had been tacked above the desk.

Pinned to a bulletin board were reminders to make calls and pay bills. There was a photo of a younger Hailey with Luna and one of the little girl with the hybrid and Paige.

Interestingly, there were no photos of Paige with Noah. No little notes or mementos of a life lived together. He'd seen a lot of homes in the course of his career, and in strong marriages there was evidence. In weaker relationships—

No. He couldn't judge Paige's marriage from the outside. Some people simply weren't sentimental.

Though Paige always had been.

Pulling out the chair, Reece sat at the desk. No stray papers littered the scarred wooden desktop. An eighteen-month desk calendar sat in the middle, featuring October of the previous year.

The month Noah had died.

Time had been short since Paige had lost her husband. Not even a year had passed. She was still grieving.

Yet another reason to keep this job professional.

Focus on work. Reece forced himself to read the calendar. In October, only one entry stood out. Three days before Noah died, a notation in one of the boxes read "WR/BC 9:00." *Wild River. Brody Carson.* Clearly, there'd been contact shortly before Noah died.

Had something tipped Brody over the edge? Maybe the animals' escape and Noah's death hadn't been an accident. It was a stretch but...

Reece flipped the page. November offered nothing.

He'd turned to December when his phone rang. Hopefully, Jodie had intel that would get him out of here before he got any more foolish ideas.

He answered the call. "Whatcha got?"

Through the line, he could hear her typing. "If you're ready, I'll start with Daniel O'Reilly, Paige's employee. He came up with a big fat nothing. Graduated from Colorado State with a degree in wildlife management. No red flags."

He'd figured as much. Lifting the calendar, he glanced under it. A manila envelope peeked from beneath. Carson Enterprises headed the return address, on Summit Street in Crystal Ridge. "How about Brody Carson?"

"I've got the most on him, so let's get the easy ones out of the way. I didn't get much on Austin Wyatt, but I can dig deeper. Even the sheriff is clean as they come."

"Maybe too clean?"

"No. There's just nothing out of the ordinary. He's pretty much always toed the line. Other than what you're telling me about him not taking the assaults on Paige seriously, he's a model sheriff."

Model sheriffs didn't dismiss those they served. "Okay, Brody then."

"Brody owns several companies and is involved in even more. They've all filed appropriate paperwork. No evidence of tax fraud or cutting corners. But one thing stands out…" She drew out the words like she wasn't quite sure what to say.

"Lay it on me." Reece was tired and discouraged, and he needed to check himself. Just because he didn't like Brody didn't mean he could invent a reason to take him down. The man might be arrogant, but that didn't make him a criminal.

"The land Howling Moon sits on, as well as the parcel beside it, were sold to Noah's great-grandfather by Brody's great-grandfather."

Reece dropped the envelope to the desk

and sat straighter in the chair. *Interesting.* "So Howling Moon is built on old Carson family land?" Land that backed up to the river. Land that was exactly what Brody had been after to run his training center.

"Appears so."

Pulling his notepad from his pocket, Reece jotted details. "Anything else?"

"Nothing important. I can send you everything I've found through secure channels."

"Sounds good."

"If I find more on Austin Wyatt, I'll pass it along." Jodie fell silent. Even her computer stilled. "Reece?"

"Yeah?" He shoved his notebook into his pocket and picked up the envelope again.

"Be careful." She killed the call before he could respond.

Was she talking about the case or about Paige?

Didn't matter. Right now, he needed to focus on Brody.

Brody. Whose company was featured in the return address on that envelope. Opening the clasp, Reece slipped the papers out. It appeared to be same contract Brody had tossed at Paige, though it was stamped "Draft" with a date two months before the other one. He flipped through the pages, scanning the parts about the mystery property. The only difference he saw was that this older version included a sale of the land to Brody and not a lease. At some point, Noah must have renegotiated, probably figuring he'd do better getting a steady income from a lease than from the one-time financial injection of a sale.

Had that angered Brody? Maybe losing his family land all over again had been too much?

Dropping the contract, Reece flipped back through the desk calendar, seeking anything that might yield more answers.

There was little of note other than scheduled vaccinations and business-related due dates. In April, one date had been highlighted in yellow and surrounded with crudely drawn stars and balloons, as though Hailey had decorated her daddy's calendar. He smiled at the childish drawings around words an adult had clearly written. *Hailey is FIVE!*

Reece dropped the calendar pages and grabbed what appeared to be an investment statement. He glanced at the bottom line, then at the account holder.

Time ground to a halt.

The account belonged to Paige, and the balance was over a hundred thousand dollars.

He gripped the papers and sank back into

the chair. The way Paige talked, the refuge had been in financial trouble almost from the start. So why was there an account with more than enough money to put the refuge in the black? To pay those back taxes on the land next door?

He skimmed the statement again and his gaze froze on the account's opening date.

It was only a couple of weeks after she'd left him.

Where had she gotten—?

No. His heart plummeted to the chair beneath him.

He looked at the calendar.

Hailey's fifth birthday was last April?

Wait. He did the math in his head, then pulled the calendar closer and verified on paper.

His gut cinched. So many things fell into place. The way his mother had behaved when Paige had left, her callous dismissals and degrading remarks. Hailey's familiar eye color, the same that looked back in the mirror at him every morning. The slight wave in her dark hair that mimicked his when it was too long. The absolute lack of Noah's features in Hailey's face.

Hailey wasn't Noah's daughter.

She was his.

Paige had thrown away their future for a bribe from his mother.

* * *

It was too dark in the house.

Paige clicked on another lamp in the living room, then stared at the window. The light only served to make the outside world seem even darker than it had been before.

She should sleep, but after their near-death experience on a twisting road, adrenaline coursed through her.

She could call Seb, but she wasn't ready to deal with what he might tell her about why Noah had kept such a huge secret from her.

The way Reece had unburdened himself to her had her brain spinning way too fast.

So was her heart. They'd talked the way they used to, when they'd held nothing back from one another. When they'd trusted one another. It had both soothed her soul and left her restless, wanting things she couldn't have. Already her chest ached and there was no doubt she'd miss him more when he returned to Denver than she ever had before.

If things were different, she could move to Denver too. Maybe resettle some of the rescues at Howling Moon with the sanctuary there. Several years ago, they'd offered her a consulting job. If she reached out, could they strike a deal now?

She sniffed and rolled her eyes. It didn't matter. She was still bound by a promise and a fear she couldn't break.

Outside, the rescues paced and refused to settle down, even though midnight had passed long ago. They were as restless as she felt. As intuitive as they tended to be, they might be picking up on her tension, even from a distance.

Either that, or something was wrong. Paige braced her hand against the wall. She couldn't handle another disaster. The thought made her bones melt.

One of them howled. Another took up the chorus.

Four days ago, she'd have grabbed her flashlight and walked out to see what was wrong. Now she was too scared to even step out onto her own porch. Terrified to descend the steps and walk into one of the enclosures.

She pulled the curtains closed and stood in the middle of the living room, her arms wrapped around her stomach, staring at the stairs to the garage. Maybe she could go down and help Reece. Surely he could use another set of eyes to—

His footsteps pounded up the stairs, heavy and quick.

Something was wrong if he was coming that fast.

Her pulse hammered so hard she could feel

it in her temples. He'd seen something suspicious. Heard something outside.

Or had he found something among Noah's business papers?

Noah, what were you involved in? She hated to think someone as kind and gentle as Noah would do something illegal to save the refuge, but he would go to great lengths to protect the people and animals he cared about. If only she—

"What is this?" Reece was speaking before he even reached the top step. He wasn't yelling, but he was definitely upset, the words animated and packed with an emotion she couldn't identify.

Paige stopped halfway to the door when Reece strode into the room carrying Noah's desk calendar and gripping a sheaf of papers. His expression wasn't that of a man who'd solved the riddle behind the violence plaguing Paige and her rescues.

No. The dark thundercloud around him bore the aura of man who'd discovered something personal. Something devastating.

Something like the truth.

Her mouth went dry. Her lips parted to explain but no words poured forth. He knew. Stepping backward, she grabbed the edge of the counter for support.

Reece slapped Noah's desk calendar on the island with one hand and slammed the papers down with the other. He braced his hands on the counter on either side of the two items and stared at them, his shoulders heaving with each breath. His lips were taut, and his jaw worked back and forth as though he was trying to force words out through the tension. His expression was tight and unreadable.

It could be anger? Or hurt?

Likely it was an icy, sickening combination of both.

Paige's feet froze to the hardwood floor. He was never supposed to know. Never supposed to find out. His mother would—

"I have no idea where to even start." His words huffed out on ragged breaths. He picked up the paper, dropped it, then ripped the top set of pages off the calendar and tossed them to the far end of the island. He stabbed a date in April with his finger.

Even from where she stood several feet away, she could see the yellow highlighter and the blocky handwriting Hailey had learned in preschool.

The memory slammed into her. The day they'd brought the calendar home from the store, Hailey had pounced. She'd planted herself at the kitchen table, made Paige mark her birthday, then snagged a highlighter laying nearby. She'd been so excited to be turning five in the next year, so wild with anticipation over going to kindergarten…

"So Pops doesn't forget." She'd scribbled back and forth so much, the highlighter had nearly bled through the paper.

Noah had laughed and ruffled her hair. "As if I could, kiddo. I have a feeling you're going to remind us plenty of times."

The childish scribble highlighted the truth she'd tried so hard to keep in the dark.

Reece was a smart man. He could count. He'd know if Hailey turned five in April then she was his daughter.

Reece's knuckles were white as he gripped the counter, his eyes fixed on the calendar. "Either I am a colossal idiot and you were somehow cheating on me with Noah the whole time or—"

"No." Everything was already shattered. She couldn't let him think she'd been unfaithful to him. That was a pain she wouldn't foist on him.

She'd loved him with everything inside her. Had trusted him. Not once had she ever violated his trust with another man. Not once had she ever even considered it. He had to know that. She forced the words out, and they fell in a whisper. "There was only you. Ever. Only you."

Reece's chin dropped. The way he stared at her. So shocked. So wounded. It nearly rocked Paige off her feet. "How could you?"

The anguish in his voice brought tears to her eyes. This was the full display of pain she'd feared for years, and it hurt worse than she'd ever imagined it could. His suffering practically slammed into her chest, seeming to fuse with the grief and secrets she'd carried for too long. It clogged her throat and dammed up her words.

She tried to breathe past the lump in her throat. "I know I hurt you. I'm sorry. Leaving you ripped me in two, but it was the only choice—"

"Don't."

He snatched up the paper and held it up between them. Even from this distance, she knew what it was. How had one of her investment statements landed in Noah's office? He'd known about the money and had agreed it should be set aside for Hailey's future. He'd insisted she needed to put the money away and then tell Reece the truth. Noah had never believed Tabitha Campbell could touch her, but he hadn't known the woman and her reputation.

Paige had dug in her heels, determined to protect Hailey's future, although she hated every penny. Together, they'd set up a trust that couldn't be touched until Hailey turned eighteen.

The page fluttered as Reece threw it onto the counter. "Did a hundred thousand make leaving hurt a little less?"

That was so low. So low, it felt as though he'd cut her off at the knees and left her bleeding.

Yes, he was hurt. Yes, she'd taken the money and vanished, but the situation was nowhere near what he must be thinking. Her actions had been purely for his benefit. If he'd ever known her at all, there was no way he could question that.

Then again, he'd probably never imagined she'd run away and marry another man either. She could make excuses all day, but in the end, the result was the same. She'd abandoned Reece without an explanation.

He deserved one now, not to assuage her guilt but to ease his pain. "You don't know what happened."

"I don't?" He finally met her eye, and the contempt in his expression nearly burned her to ashes. "Why don't you tell me? Because it looks to me like my mother dangled one of her famous *make the problem go away* carrots in your face and you bit."

He knew the money came from his mother? One of the reasons she'd fled was to spare him the truth about his family. A truth he seemed to have learned anyway.

Still, even with all that had happened to his family, she didn't want to talk about that day. Couldn't stand to remember how it felt to be dismissed and discarded, both she and their unborn child. "I did it for Hailey."

"You stole my daughter."

Paige opened her mouth and closed it again. There was no argument. No way to make it better.

Reece wasn't thinking rationally at the moment anyway. His emotions were running the show. Maybe he'd calm down. Maybe later—

A gunshot rattled the windows.

Paige dropped to her knees and covered her head as the animals howled in frantic fear.

FOURTEEN

"Paige!" Reece half ran, half slid to where Paige had dropped to the floor on the other side of the island, putting himself between her and the window. He hadn't heard glass shatter, but had she been hit?

Maverick raced to his side, alert and ready.

From somewhere on the far side of the animal enclosures, an alarm blared. Its echo ricocheted off the hill, chasing the gunshot.

"I'm fine." Paige stood and shoved Reece out of the way, seeming to ignore the gunshot. "That alarm. It's the back gate behind the barn. Noah installed it after someone made off with his four-wheeler a couple of years ago. It leads to the path that goes up the hill and runs behind the fences." She stalked to the door, stopping only long enough to grab her boots.

"You are not going out there." Had she lost

her grip on reality? Someone was on the property with what sounded like a rifle. There was no way she was plunging into the darkness with no knowledge of where the shooter was or who they were targeting.

She whirled on him, her eyes wide and her expression tight. "Reece, if someone got past that entrance, they can open the emergency gates along the back sides of each enclosure. Those gates are there in case we have to let the hybrids loose in a wildfire." She balanced on one foot to tug on her boot. "In about one minute, someone can have every single one of my animals loose and running the hills. You think Brody Carson won't amp up his fear campaign in town and shut me down for good then? Or worse…" She shifted to the other foot and pulled on her other boot "He's got enough people terrified of my rescues that it wouldn't take much for a spooked homeowner to shoot on sight."

"Paige…" He was speaking to the wind. She was already out the door.

While he might be furious and hurt, there was no way he could stand by and watch her throw herself into danger.

He took the outside steps two at a time with Maverick on his heels as Paige rounded the barn. She was fast. Adrenaline drove her forward.

The alarm blared louder outside, the overlapping echoes tearing at his ears as though they were alive and working with all of their might to confuse his senses. He glanced at the enclosures as he ran after Paige. Not a single one of the wolf hybrids was in sight. Something was definitely wrong. He drew his sidearm and crept forward.

Sudden silence descended on the refuge as the last echo of the alarm died. Paige must have reached the fence. He needed to get to her quickly. Whoever had fired that shot was still—

A scream tore through the darkness, replacing the shriek of the alarm.

"Paige!" He pushed forward, rounding the barn so fast he skidded on loose gravel and went down to one knee. Scrambling up, he stopped. It was too dark back here. The light over the barn's rear door was out. Probably the result of the gunshot they'd heard earlier.

Whoever was on the property didn't want to be seen.

Reece and Maverick were moving targets silhouetted against the lights from the driveway and the house. Whoever was out in the darkness could see him, but aside from moving tree shadows in the breeze, he could see nothing.

He couldn't protect himself by taking cover,

not with Paige in danger. He edged forward in the darkness with Maverick, trying to keep to the narrow shadow where the lights from the front of the barn didn't reach the hard-packed dirt. He bit his tongue to keep from calling out for Paige. She had to be here somewhere. She had to be alive.

If she wasn't…

If she wasn't, then the last thing they'd shared would be his accusations and his anger. He'd been justified, yes, but if she was gone, he wasn't sure—

Stop. He exhaled slowly and put one foot in front of the other with cautious deliberation, scanning the shadows as his eyes adjusted. *Head over heart. Head over heart.* The words pounded with his pulse. He had to focus or they were both lost.

The fence gradually seemed to melt out of the darkness. The gate hung half open.

A shadowed mass lay tumbled on the ground in the opening.

Paige.

Gun aimed low, Reece approached, forcing himself to scan the surrounding area for threats as he neared her motionless form. Nothing moved.

A truck's engine revved and tires spun on

gravel. Reece whipped around, trying to orient himself and to locate the sound. The logging road. Whoever had come onto the property had parked there, out of sight, and slipped in under the cover of night and trees.

Now they were gone.

Praying he was right and no one had remained behind to fire another shot, he holstered his pistol and dropped to his knees, reaching for Paige. *Lord, please. Please let her be okay.*

His hand brushed her shoulder and she rocketed up, flailing at him with both fists. "Stop! Why are you doing this?"

"Paige. It's me." He ducked her swinging fists and grabbed her hands. "It's Reece. You're safe."

She visibly deflated. Her shoulders slumped. She sank against Reece's chest, her fists balled against his stomach. "The rescues are gone. At least four of them are gone."

"You're sure?" She'd only been a few seconds ahead of him with no time to check the enclosures.

While the animals were secondary to her safety, he needed to hear her out. As much as he wanted to know if she'd been injured, she'd never tell him until she'd first focused on the rescues she loved.

"Yes. I saw them bolt right before I got hit."

"What happened to you?"

She sniffed, but there were no tears. Slowly, she pulled away from him and laid her hand at the back of her head. Even in the near-darkness, her face was pale. "Someone hit me after I turned off the alarm. I think…" She met his eyes, hers wide with a mix of fear and pain and anger. "I think they'd have hit me again if you hadn't yelled my name." She breathed in a shaky breath and turned to the gate. "Whoever it was ran off."

He drew her to him and held her close. The danger had likely passed. She was safe for the moment.

While his head screamed her betrayal, his heart beat with relief. They could hash out the past when this was over.

When his daughter was safe. The swirl of emotions exploded again. He was a father. A father who had missed a huge chunk of his daughter's life, when she'd passed so many milestones and formed so many bonds. His thoughts swirled until he wasn't even sure what he felt anymore.

Except for one thing. He was swamped by an overwhelming desire to stand here with Paige in his arms forever, shielding her and keeping her safe. No, it was more. He wanted to comfort her and to be comforted by her.

It made no sense. She was the one who'd cut him to the core and yet...

She was the one he wanted to talk it out with. How was that possible?

He deliberately shelved his wants in favor of their needs. Danger was still out there. If he hadn't followed Paige, it was likely someone would have crushed her skull and—

Head over heart.

His arms tightened around Paige briefly and he let her go, walking toward the fence. "Maverick. Search." His sharp command set the K-9 into motion. He sniffed around the gate, returning to sit by Reece's side.

Nothing.

If only his partner had been trained to track.

Paige pulled the back of his shirt. "We have to go find the escapees. If someone in town spots them or Brody finds out they're loose, this will all be over. The only thing I've had going for me this past year is none of them escaped. Now?"

Now the animals were running the hills. Their night of freedom would give Brody the final play, turning public sentiment firmly against Paige.

"Is there somewhere specific they'd go?" Surely, they wouldn't roam too far from food and shelter. Then again, they were half domestic and half wild. Even Paige had said it could be hard to predict what they'd do.

"Havoc was leading the pack. He's the escape artist. He got out several times before Noah and Daniel reinforced the fences, and each time he headed in the same direction. They likely went over the hill and along the river near where Brody wanted to build his rafting school. Last time, we found them about a mile downriver on the other side of the rapids where—" She turned and walked toward the house. "There's a raft in the barn, already on the trailer. We can tow it to the river and see if they went that way again."

How many times was he going to have to pull her away from the edge? Noah had died on the very rapids she wanted to navigate in the dark of night and in the heat of the moment. Reece caught up to her and kept pace beside her. "How much do you know about rafting? In the dark?"

"By the time we gear up and get to the landing, it will be close to dawn. Noah trained me well. Even with the rain, the river shouldn't be high. You're talking class two rapids at the worst. Nothing we can't handle."

"Paige…"

"You don't understand." She stopped and whirled toward him. "I will not go down like this. I'm not going to lose my home. Hailey's home. I'm not going to let my daughter—"

"Our daughter."

Paige flinched.

He shouldn't have said it. Now wasn't the time, but it rose up in him with a fierce new protectiveness like he'd never felt before. He had a daughter. That little girl carried his DNA. This wasn't just about Paige and her rescues. It was about his child as well. "We'll fight together." As much as he didn't want to go on this foolhardy rescue attempt, he'd do what it took to maintain a sense of security in Hailey's life.

Paige's mouth opened then closed. For the briefest moment, it seemed she forgot the urgency of the situation as regret crossed her face.

Abruptly, she turned and started walking again, pulling her phone out of her pocket as she jogged to the house. She punched a button. "Daniel. Somebody released Havoc and three of the others. I couldn't see which ones. Reece and I are taking the raft out to get them. Can you come back and check the fence line?" She listened, nodded, then pressed the screen and shoved the phone back into her pocket as they reached the large door at the front of the barn.

"What do you want me to do?" Reece felt helpless and lost. He knew nothing of rafting or rapids. This was Paige's show to run.

"Clear anything blocking the trailer. I'll get the truck and—"

A truck's engine roared up the driveway, and headlights bounced between the trees.

Reece stepped in front of Paige as the truck skidded to a stop, spitting gravel against the side of the house. He rested his hand on his pistol, his heart pounding. Whoever had attacked Paige had returned to finish what they'd started.

"Paige!" Austin Wyatt roared in a way Paige had never heard him yell before. He stalked away from his truck, the headlights outlining him like he was a serial killer in a horror movie poster. When he was close enough for the barn lights to highlight his features, his eyes were murderous. "It's gone too far this time."

Paige planted her feet and tried to find some balance. This whole night was off kilter. Austin was pushy but soft-spoken. Witnessing anger in him quaked her stomach, although she refused to let him see it.

Before she could respond, Reece strode over. "I'd agree. This is too far." Reece stepped between Paige and the rancher. "If you came back to finish what you started—"

"What are you talking about?" Confusion replaced the ire in Austin's expression but then he shook his head as if to clear it and aimed a finger over Reece's shoulder at Paige. "Your wolves killed two of my cattle. Callie found them and told me. You're—"

No way was she going to stand by for this kind of accusation. "What makes you think my rescues are involved?"

"We haven't had coyotes or wolves around here in ages. Your beasts are the only ones that could have done it. I'm through defending you. I'll have you shut down by morning."

Oh no he wouldn't. The chaos of the night ran through her, but her whiplashing emotions stilled into determination. Nobody threatened her or her rescues.

She shoved Reece aside and went nose-to-chin with Austin. "You have no proof." She stopped short of shoving her finger into his chest. "Unless you want me to bring you up on trespassing charges, you'll leave now."

"Like the sheriff would ever believe you." Austin's voice dripped derision.

"He's the least of your worries." From behind her, Reece's voice came low and hard. "The last thing you want is a federal charge, Mr. Wyatt. I suggest you do as Paige asks."

Austin's nostrils flared. It almost looked as though he considered charging around Paige to confront Reece. Instead, he backed off and shoved a finger a mere inch from her nose. "This ends in the morning." With a sneer, he stalked to his truck and spun out in a hail of gravel.

Paige balled her fists and turned away from the dirt and rock raining over her.

How did Austin even know her rescues had escaped? Maybe Brody wasn't the culprit after all.

Until she found the animals, there was no time to ponder. Without looking at Reece, she went to the house to retrieve her truck. In short order, she'd hitched the trailer and raft and was navigating the driveway toward the one-lane dirt road to the river. Why had she never asked why the two properties were connected? Why Noah could access the river whenever he wanted? "Why didn't he tell me?"

Remembering Noah and considering his lie of omission wasn't exactly what she needed, especially not with Reece riding shotgun and

Maverick on the seat between them. Not when she'd committed an even bigger omission.

Noah had hidden land. Paige had hidden a child.

"I don't know." Reece's voice was low, and it was obvious he wasn't talking about Noah's silence.

She wanted to tell him the whole truth, but now wasn't the time. Hailey was the bigger matter, but her animals were the more pressing.

It was doubtful they'd ever regain their footing with one another. Reece wasn't likely to trust her again. There was so much to say, but Reece deserved more than she could give him in this predawn rush to the river.

The truck bounced into a rut. Paige jerked the wheel, pulling her focus back to the present. Navigating the river at dawn was not her wisest decision ever, but it was all she had.

She gripped the wheel tighter. While she loved the river, she hadn't been rafting since the day Noah died. Now here she was, preparing to navigate the very stretch of water that had stolen him away.

God, I can't take any more. Please. Hold me together.

At the small beach Noah used to put the raft in the water, Paige maneuvered the truck into position and shut off the engine. "There are life jackets and helmets in the raft."

The sky above them softened with early morning light, gradually bringing the world into view. Birds took up their morning songs, a joyful noise at odds with the gravity of their situation.

The songs were a reminder God was still God. He held Paige and Hailey and Reece, and even the rescues, in the palm of His hand.

In silence, they strapped on life preservers and helmets. Paige gave Reece a quick rundown of what to expect as they navigated the rapids.

She eyed the water as they prepared to shove off. It was slightly higher than she'd expected, but nothing like the raging force that had swamped Noah's raft. Paige studied the swift flow, confident in her ability to navigate, even with an untested copilot.

"You're thinking something." Reece stood beside her, also watching the water. "It's moving fast."

"Nothing unusual." Paige adjusted the straps on her life jacket and helmet. "We used to go rafting often. Hailey, too, if we were hitting a class one." She waved a hand for him to help her slide the raft into the water. "Just remembering."

With a curt nod, Reece bent his back to the job of getting them afloat. They paddled downstream, letting the river carry them as Paige guided them along the current. The water was swift but smooth. In about a mile, that would change. Hopefully, they'd spot the animals before they reached rapids.

Muscles that had long been unused began to scream. Paige's head ached from the blow she'd taken earlier, the one she hadn't fully described to Reece. Her wounded shoulder protested and the rest of her body joined the chorus. This was so much more physically taxing than she'd remembered.

Her training kicked in, and she instinctively guided the craft, watching the current and hidden objects as Reece and Maverick eyed the banks. She kept up a steady stream of prayer. Occasionally, Reece's muttering drifted to her. No doubt, he was praying as well.

Maverick watched the riverbank as though he understood what he was searching for. He was one more distraction, though. She'd never had a dog in the boat, and her stomach tensed at the idea of him pitching over the side.

But Maverick was well-trained and sure-footed. He'd be fine. He had to be. She couldn't be responsible for Reece losing his partner.

As the darkness continued to retreat, the light in the river valley began to shift, providing clearer vision.

The sound of the river changed too. In the near distance, the first set of rapids was a dull roar over the rocks.

The same rocks had spun Noah's raft and tossed him overboard. The county coroner said head trauma had killed him instantly.

Paige gripped the paddle tighter. It was her job to get them through. She couldn't dwell on the past or on missing the man who had been her best friend and closest confidant. Nor could she dwell on the man in front of her.

Her focus needed to be on the river ahead of her…and the God above her.

The river was choppier than she'd expected, the water piling up behind rocks and racing over them along channels that had shifted and moved since she'd last been in the area with. In the early morning light, she scanned the way the water moved and chose a channel to slide through, noting an eddy in the middle that could spin them sideways.

This would take all of her know-how and all of Reece's strength as he worked in front of her.

"Tell Maverick to stay down, then paddle like you've never paddled before. Trust me to steer." She had to raise her voice over the water.

Reece looked over his shoulder at his partner. "Maverick. Down."

The dog immediately dropped behind Reece, his back pressed against Reece's life jacket.

They hit the rapids suddenly, the rear of the raft skidding sideways. Paige dug her paddle in and rowed, pumping against the current to turn the nose of the boat toward the next slip in the stream.

In front of her, Reece drove his paddle into the water even faster than she did, keeping the raft moving steadily.

Maverick fixed his eyes on.

They slipped neatly between two rocks, and Paige shifted sides, preparing to navigate the next shift in the current. Two more changes, and they'd be free.

She focused on the route, ignoring her brain as it tried to scan the rocks for the one that had ended Noah's life. That wasn't—

Maverick struggled to his feet with a sharp bark, his attention on the bank to their right.

At the edge of the water, the four escapees stood grouped together and watching the raft's progress.

Relief washed through Paige. The animals were safe. All she had to do was get them to the bank. Then she could call Daniel and—

The raft jolted and rocked sideways from the middle.

Maverick barked and staggered.

Paige dug in and fought against the spin that threatened to pitch them all into the water.

The raft lurched.

There was a yelp. Maverick rolled over the side into the foaming rapids and disappeared beneath the water.

FIFTEEN

Reece dug his paddle in, ears attuned for instructions from Paige as he pushed forward, praying his seemingly fruitless efforts would help her keep them upright and moving toward smoother path ahead. The last jolt had nearly thrown him from the raft, and he pressed himself deeper into the small craft, determined not to pitch headfirst into the water on the receiving end of a rescue they didn't need to attempt.

On the bank, the missing rescues watched, seemingly entertained by their struggle. *Lord, let them stay there.* If they fled into the woods, this entire trek would have to start all over. Paige would be devastated.

They needed a win.

He paddled harder, driving for the calm water only feet away.

"Maverick!" Paige's frantic cry stuttered Reece's motion to a stop as they finally edged out of the rapids into still water. He dropped his paddle into the raft and turned, no longer feeling Maverick's weight pressed against his back.

Paige was leaning over the back of the boat, her paddle abandoned, scrambling in the water. "Reece! Maverick went overboard!"

His jaw tightened until his temples ached. As the raft slipped gently sideways, he scrambled toward Paige, rocking the small craft as they drifted slowly away from the rapids. "Where?" He had to get to his partner, had to rescue him, even if it meant diving in and swimming against the current into the eddying flow that had nearly defeated them the first time.

Pointing a trembling finger toward the rock that must have bucked the raft, she leaned forward, searching the rapids, nearly pitching in headfirst.

Reece grabbed for her, frantically wrapping his fingers into the strap of her life jacket. "Don't need you over the side, too." He muttered the words under his breath as he scanned the churning water for his partner. Where was he? "Maverick!"

"There!" Paige jerked free of his grasp and swung her arm to the right, where the rapids faded into smooth water.

A sodden mass of fur struggled out of the

water onto the opposite bank and laid there, panting heavily.

Reece almost caved over on himself in relief. His partner was safe. Soaking wet and exhausted, but safe.

"Maverick. Stay!"

The K-9 didn't even acknowledge Reece's shouted command. Likely, he was worn out and a little scared. Maverick was probably perfectly happy to stay right where he was in the warm sunbeam. Worn out but alive.

"How do we get to him?" He turned to Paige. This was her wheelhouse. As much as he wanted to dive into the water and swim across, that would be a foolish endeavor.

She looked over her shoulder at the four animals on the bank behind them, still watching with interest. Then she turned and looked at Maverick. The decisions in her mind played out on her face. There was a choice to be made here. Both of them knew it.

Drawing her lips between her teeth, Paige reached down and picked up her paddle. "It's calm enough here to paddle across and get Mav. We'll get him to the raft and then go back for the rest of the pack."

"Will they wait?" There was no doubt Paige's heart would shatter if those animals took off again. They were so close. If the rescues bolted, then they'd lose their shot to corral them and get them back to Howling Moon. If that happened, it would be more devastating to Paige than the initial discovery they were missing.

"If they think I have food with me, they'll wait." She jerked her chin toward the front of the raft and shoved her paddle into the water. "Paddle on the right side. Maverick might be injured, so he takes priority."

Reece obeyed, keeping his eye on his partner as they traversed the calmer water on this side of the rapids.

She was choosing him over herself. Putting his partner before the animals she loved.

Had that been what she was doing when she'd left? Putting him first? Maybe she hadn't viewed her actions as abandonment but as protection.

Betrayed anger zipped through him, but it faded as quickly as it hit. He needed to hear all of her heart, not just the little bit he'd let her speak a few hours before.

They'd talk this out. She'd explain. He'd—

He had no idea what he'd do. Beyond praying the same prayers he'd been praying since he'd spotted her lying in a heap by the gate. *Help me do the right thing, Lord.* With his head and his heart at war, it was all he knew to pray.

The bank gently sloped away from the river in a spot between the rocks, and Paige steered them in that direction. Reece splashed into the water as soon as he felt the raft scrape bottom and pulled with all his might to get the craft onto shore.

He didn't wait for Paige. Maverick needed him. If his partner was injured, it was all his fault. He should have been watching him, paying attention to what was happening. Maybe he never should have brought him along on this search at all.

By the time he ran back, Maverick had risen to greet Reece on shaky legs.

Reece dropped to his knees beside the shepherd. "Hey, buddy. You okay?"

Maverick responded with a rare lick up Reece's cheek, then shook from tail to head, water flying everywhere. The action nearly dropped the K-9 to the rocky ground, but he recovered his footing before he went down.

Unfastening Maverick's harness, Reece scanned the dog then ran his hands over his joints, back and belly, searching for injuries. Other than the shakiness of his overexertion and the adrenaline from his battle against the current, Maverick appeared to be unharmed.

Thank you, Lord. So much. People often

failed to understand Maverick was more than a pet. He was a partner. A friend. A fellow officer. To lose him to the river would have been—

Reece took a calming breath. He hadn't been lost. He was safe.

And they had a job to do.

He looked down at Maverick. "Let's go." Together, they turned toward the raft.

Reece nearly collided with Paige, who stood right behind him.

"Is Maverick okay?" The stress of the ordeal rattled her voice.

He wanted to comfort her and confront her all at the same time. As soon as this was over, they had to talk. He couldn't live with these dueling emotions. Loving her meant forgiving her, but how did a man forgive a woman who'd—

"Reece?" She leaned to peer around him at his partner. "Is he okay?"

For the millionth time, he reminded himself to focus. "Tired, but he appears to be fine. Let's get back across before your wolf-dogs take off on us again."

He didn't have to tell her twice. She turned and hurried to the raft. In short order, they had the boat back in the river and were paddling across the calmer water, though they had to fight the current to keep from sweeping down-stream.

The four rescues paced the bank, keeping even with the raft as it approached.

When Paige found a spot to beach the craft, the animals backed away to the edge of the trees but remained close.

Ordering Maverick to stay, Reece jumped from the raft and helped Paige pull it to shore. "Why aren't they bolting?" They'd taken off from Howling Moon at the first whiff of freedom. Why not go all the way? Even some of the RMKU's K-9 trainees would choose wide open spaces over the roomiest enclosure when they were first brought into the program.

"Food." Paige flashed a grin despite the situation. "They see me, they're reminded of how easy it is to eat when I'm around. No hunting. No tracking." She shoved straggling wet hair away from her face and turned to the animals. "It's hard to know with hybrids what you'll get. Some have the tamer dog side take over. Others have the wilder wolf side overpower the DNA. Those are the ones that tend to get into trou-ble. This crew seems slightly more content to be pampered." Retrieving a large duffel from where she'd lashed it into the raft, she went up the slight incline to the animals, who gathered around her, sniffing the bag she carried.

Reece hung back when the small pack eyed him with suspicion. The last thing he wanted was to send them bounding into the woods where they might never be found again. He'd seen enough to know if Paige couldn't account for every one of the rescues in her care, Brody Carson would use the missing animals to incite fears of wild, rabid wolves hunting down innocent prey.

Nothing could be further from the truth. Paige plopped down in the middle of them and pulled a huge plastic container from her bag. Opening it, she dumped a pile of dry food in front of each of the animals who nudged and pushed at her. As they ate, she pulled several long leads from the bag and clipped them to each collar, securing them to some sort of spike she screwed into the softer ground where she'd settled.

It was clear by the way the animals behaved that it was about more than food when it came to Paige. They loved her. Protected her. After a gray-and-white hybrid and a brown-and-white one had finished eating, they sat in front of Paige with their back to her, watching him, protecting her from the threat they perceived him to be.

Maybe it was because they didn't really

know him. Maybe it was because Maverick made them antsy. Or maybe they could feel the tension inside him and knew it had to do with Paige.

Either way, he settled in with Maverick at his side about fifteen feet away, close enough to speak but far enough to keep the animals relaxed.

Paige pulled her phone from a waterproof pouch on the side of the bag. "I'm sending our location to Daniel so he can get close with the truck. There's a trail he can get down about a quarter of a mile from here. He'll walk in, take two of the hybrids while I take the other two, and we'll hike them to the truck, then you and I can get the raft down to the next landing." She tucked the phone into her pocket and stared at the animals in front of her. "You're smart to stay back. They're keyed up from their adventure."

Adventure? According to Austin Wyatt, they'd killed two of his cattle. That was more than an *adventure*. That was a big issue she was going to have to address. "What do you plan to do about Austin?"

Her nostrils flared. She reached over and scratched the ears of the animal closest to her, pressed against her leg like a massive lap dog.

They looked as far from wild hunters as canines could get.

"Either Austin's lying or someone set up my rescues. They weren't out ten minutes before he showed up at the house, and we found them here, in the complete opposite direction of the ranch. Animals don't kill for a thrill. They kill to eat. These guys had no need to attack and, if they had, they'd have been caught feeding on the cattle. They also didn't have time to make it this far down the river if they went that way first." She shook her head. "No, someone's lying. They want something from me. At this point, they won't stop until either me or my animals are dead."

"I'm not going to let that happen." Reece stood and walked to the riverbank, looking upstream as though he expected an attack. He stood tall, but something was different.

Something in him seemed defeated. He'd worn that same air since he'd stomped up from the garage demanding answers.

Answers she needed to give him. She shifted, feeling suddenly antsy, and reached for Havoc, who trotted over and laid down with his head in Paige's lap.

Paige buried her fingers in the dog's neck

fur. "Reece?" If only her voice didn't sound so thin and uncertain.

He must have heard the shift in her tone, because he turned slowly. It was almost as though he expected her to land a punch, even though she sat a fair distance away.

It could be considered an emotional punch, maybe.

Paige sighed. The truth had been wedged inside of her so long, it might not come out without a whole lot more effort and energy than she had left in her.

But it had to. "You deserve the truth."

He inhaled a shaky breath and held her gaze as if trying to read whether or not she would really come clean with the past. At her slight nod, he sat on a rock to his left and rested his elbows on his knees. He was trying to look relaxed, but the way he laced his fingers and held tight gave him away.

Maverick seemed to sense his tension and paced over to lay between him and Paige. Guess even he thought there was some sort of threat in the words she needed to say.

Paige wasn't even sure where to start. At the beginning? With Quentin? Or straight to the center of everything with his mother's rejection and treachery?

Before she could start her story though, Reece spoke. "Why didn't you tell me about Hailey?" The question and the anguish in his voice was almost more than she could absorb.

Yet she couldn't fall into emotion. She had to find a place inside her that could deal in facts, in truth, and not in the pain they'd all endured.

He deserved the entire story, even the ugly parts. No holding back. No more protecting his family.

No more protecting herself.

She swallowed the tears that wanted to choke her words. "When I left your house that night, I suspected…" Looking down at Havoc, she tried to draw courage from pale blue eyes that always seemed to want the best for her. "I bought a pregnancy test on the way home and it was positive."

"So you knew you were pregnant when you left." His voice was hollow.

"I did."

"And you ran to Noah?" He threw his hands out to the sides. "That's the part I don't understand." Standing, he paced to the river, staring upstream. Hands planted on his hips, he finally faced her. "Why, Paige?"

"Noah was a good friend in high school, and we'd kept in touch. He had just found out he had

Huntington's disease. Over time, it would rob him of… Well, it would steal everything about him mentally and physically. He needed someone to help him. We were friends before we married, and we were friends after. He never asked for more of me and I never asked for more of him. Reece, I had nowhere else to go."

"You had me." He was emphatic, although his voice was ragged. "I loved you. I'd have done anything for you. I'd have—"

"Destroyed your family for me?"

His jaw slackened, and something seemed to click. "What do you mean?" He stepped closer and almost reached for her, but he stopped halfway. "Quentin did something. What's the whole truth? You said he didn't lay a hand on you, but there's more to it, isn't there?"

Shaking her head, she held up her hands to stop his words. It was harder to say than she'd imagined. The fear was very real. "He never touched me. I promise. He…" *He just threatened to.* Really, did Reece need to hear what he already knew? "He came to my apartment with some friends. I wouldn't let them in. But I was still holding the pregnancy test, and Quentin isn't stupid."

"But he *is* mean." Reece dragged his hand

down his face. "You turned him down, so he retaliated."

"He told your mother I was pregnant." Now that she'd opened the gates to the truth, the words flowed more easily. The jagged edges tore at her throat, but they poured forth freely.

"She bought you off." Turning, he stalked to the river. "You walked away with our daughter for…what? A hundred grand? I still can't believe you had a price."

"I didn't." Her voice was so low, so empty. "You know I loved you. That I wanted a family with you. That—"

"Then why?"

"Because of Quentin." The words ripped out loud enough to lift the heads of every animal lying around them. "Because of your mother. Because I couldn't live in fear of him and I couldn't stay when your mother hated me. I couldn't live with myself if I divided a family. I had nothing and no one growing up. I was used to being on my own. You had everything. Two parents, a brother, the legendary white picket fence… I wasn't going to be the one responsible for stealing that from you."

"Stealing it from me?" His brow wrinkled. "Paige." There was a different emotion in his voice this time. Something tender. Something quiet. "You couldn't steal what my mother and Quentin had already destroyed. We didn't realize it at the time, but my family was falling to pieces long before I met you. It would have collapsed whether you stayed or not." His shoulders heaved. "You banked that money for Hailey, didn't you?"

"I did. Your mother said if I ever reached out to you or told you, then she'd take the money and…and Hailey." This time, her voice cracked. Now that he knew everything, the freedom in her chest was overwhelming. The wall around her heart shattered and she knew with all that was in her…

She loved Reece Campbell. From the moment he'd stepped back into her life, she'd known. With the fear gone and the truth exposed, fresh air hit emotions and banked embers flamed to life.

It was true she'd loved Noah. She'd been the best wife she could be to him given the platonic nature of their marriage. Had been totally faithful. Had never let her thoughts or emotions stray toward Reece.

Reece Campbell wasn't the one who got away. This wasn't the Reece she'd once known, returning to pick up where they'd left off. She had fallen for the man he was now. The protector. The defender. The honorable man who would sacrifice himself to protect the innocent. The man she'd wounded, and whose family had dug the knife in deeper, but whose scars had made him resilient and empathetic and strong.

"I wish you had told me sooner." When Reece finally met her gaze, his expression was unreadable. "I'd have understood. I'd have shielded you. We could have—"

"Would you?" Paige wasn't so sure. "You had no idea back then what your brother was capable of and no idea your mother was so ruthless. I was the outsider. I knew you loved me, but did you love me enough?" She gestured to stem his argument before he could start it, tears stinging the back of her nose. "I needed to be here with Noah. To find myself, and what I truly love. To learn what it means to sacrificially love someone else and how to accept love in return. Noah needed me. I needed him and the rescues at Howling Moon. Because of him and these animals, I learned how to love others and myself. It hurt us both when I ran, but eventually I'd have run out of fear. Out of thinking I wasn't good enough for you. Better I did it then than after we were married."

Maybe that was the purpose of her time at Howling Moon. Not to rescue, but to be rescued.

"So what now?" He looked at her like he wanted her to move closer. "Because I do know. And you will never have to worry about her again. She can't hurt you now. She can't steal Hailey or her future."

But what about their future? Together? Was he waiting for her to say something?

Was she brave enough to say the words? To go all-in with a man who would give her all of himself with a passion she'd never had with Noah? To truly pour all of herself into him? "I—"

"Paige!" A voice ripped from the tree line and echoed off the hillside. The four rescues and Maverick all sprang to attention, facing the approaching figure.

Daniel.

They were rescued... But did she want to be?

With a last long look at Reece, she pressed Pause on their future in favor of immediate need. They'd finish this conversation later and, for now, that was enough.

Reece shrugged, his face tight with regret, and walked to the raft, probably to grab his gear.

As Daniel's footsteps crunched closer, she stepped toward the path that wound between the trees. "You're a sight for sore eyes. How far are you parked from—" The words caught in her throat and nearly gagged her.

As Daniel broke through the trees, his arm rose and he leveled a pistol…

…straight at Paige's head.

SIXTEEN

"Daniel."

At Paige's gasped exclamation, Reece whirled to find the young man standing near Paige with a pistol aimed shakily at her.

Reece's hand automatically reached for his gun, but Daniel saw the movement.

"Do not." His gaze flicked to Reece and back to Paige. "If you touch that pistol, I'll put a stop to this right here." His voice wavered and his hand shook.

This was bad. Really bad. The kid wasn't a calm and collected killer, but that made everything worse. If he got too twitchy, chances were high his trigger finger would end everything even if he never intended to hurt Paige.

Raising her hands to shoulder height, Paige backed away from Daniel, stumbling over one of the rescues who stood behind her. She righted herself, never taking her eyes off her trusted employee. "Tell me what's going on, Daniel. We can work through it." Her voice was remarkably calm.

Reece pulled his gaze from the gun to assess the situation. He released a shaky breath. Seemed as though Paige might be steadier than he was.

Good. She could keep Daniel occupied while he came up with a plan to turn the gun away from her. Hopefully, she'd keep the kid dialoguing.

"I don't understand, Daniel." She eased back again, moving subtly in Reece's direction.

Smart. Since Reece was armed, Daniel would likely focus on what he was doing without realizing Paige was doing the moving for him. *Keep it up, Paige. Keep it up.*

Beside her, Havoc rose and pressed against her leg, growling low in his throat as his hackles raised. He strained toward Daniel, but the lead attached to his collar held him back.

Daniel glanced at the animal. "Knock it off, Havoc. You know me."

"But he doesn't know you stressed out like this." Paige's foot slipped back another inch. "He can probably feel your tension, hear the tone in your voice, and he doesn't like it." Reaching down, she grabbed Havoc's collar and pulled him closer, managing to gain another foot of ground toward Reece as she drew the dog away from Daniel.

Havoc snarled, baring teeth in a way that chilled Reece's blood. For the first time, he understood Paige's assertion that the hybrids could fall to the tame dog side or unpredictably to the wild wolf side.

Around their makeshift camp, the other three rescues stood, but they clustered to one side between Reece and Paige. It was almost as though they'd bolt into the woods at the first opportunity if they weren't tied down.

If they weren't tied down. Like the sun coming over the mountains and illuminating their way earlier in the day, light dawned in Reece's thoughts.

Paige was smart. Really smart.

Reece held his hands out to his sides, waiting for his moment. If he was right about Paige's plan and it actually worked, they might get out of this alive.

If Daniel didn't twitch that trigger first. Reece was finding it hard not to focus on that shaking hand. His silent prayers fell over one another and blended with his thoughts as he tried to create an exit plan.

"Tell me why you're doing this." Another

backward step. "I thought you loved the refuge and the animals. I thought—"

"Stop!" Daniel jerked the gun higher.

Reece flinched, waiting for the gunshot that didn't come.

"There are things I love more, okay?" Daniel's voice shook, but his shout echoed off the rocks. "You should have sold when you had the chance. Now... Now I don't know."

There was a hopelessness in Daniel's voice that forced Reece's plans into overdrive. He talked like someone who was at the last resort. He had to know that, even if he let Paige live, he'd clearly implicated himself in all of the attacks, including his own.

So why hadn't he fired?

Because he was scared. Frightened people did things without thinking of the consequences.

It was now or never. Careful to keep his hands away from his gun, Reece stepped forward, motioning for Maverick to follow. While Maverick wasn't trained to attack, he was trained to protect Reece. That might be what saved them now.

Reece cleared his throat and Daniel's gaze flickered to him. "Don't come closer."

"Look, man." Reece kept inching forward.

"I can get you out of this without you having to hurt anybody."

"Too late." The shaking in Daniel's hand increased with his agitation as he tried to watch both Paige and Reece. "You're a cop. You won't forget what you're seeing right now. If I want this to work… If I want—" He shook his head fiercely, swinging the gun toward Reece and lowering it to aim at his heart. "You have to die."

Reece dropped to his knees suddenly, groaning as if he'd been hit. *Come on, Mav...*

When Daniel stepped closer and loomed over him, Maverick leaped.

The massive weight of the dog's body knocked Daniel off balance. He shouted as he stumbled back, the gun bouncing on the ground at his feet. His head hit rock and he lay still.

As Maverick stood over Daniel, Reece scrambled kicked the gun out of reach, then drew his SIG, leveling it at Daniel.

Paige fell backward, dragging Havoc with her. Landing on her backside, Paige drew the dog close and buried her face in his neck, muffling what sounded like sobs.

Reece would comfort her in a moment. Holstering his sidearm, he commanded Maverick to sit and then rolled Daniel onto his stomach.

He pulled zip ties from his thigh pocket and restrained the younger man, who was barely conscious but seemed to be stable.

When he turned to Paige, Havoc bared his teeth, still in protective mode.

Reece retreated slowly until he was past the length of Havoc's lead. "Are you okay?"

Lifting her chin, Paige nodded and swiped tears from her face. She glanced at Daniel. "Is he…"

"He's alive. As soon as he comes to, we'll get him and the dogs out of here, then I'm calling for backup and paying a visit to the Flying W."

Paige looked away from Daniel, who moaned slightly and tried to rise before sinking to the ground again. "You heard that, too?"

"The line about you selling? Yeah, I heard it." Loud and clear. Austin Wyatt was their man. Reece wrestled aside the growing anger he felt at the man who had lied about running them off the road and who had attempted to terrorize Paige only a couple of hours earlier. He'd have to be calm when he made the arrest. Hopefully, Daniel would take a plea deal and would give them a confession pointing directly to the rancher.

As the other rescues ventured closer to Paige, seeking comfort, she reached for them. "What did he mean by there are things he loves more than the rescues?"

Reece had no idea, but that statement had been chasing around his thoughts as well. "Money?"

"No." Daniel stirred and tried to sit up, but with his hands behind his back, he was unsuccessful.

Leaning down, Reece helped him up and steadied him. "Then what?"

Daniel's glare was so full of hatred that Paige flinched. He shifted away and refused to speak again.

"Let's go." Reece pulled Daniel toward the trail and the younger man stumbled forward. "We'll come back for the raft. Can you handle the rescues?"

"Let me walk ahead of you so they're not seeing Daniel the whole time and we should be fine."

Reece tugged Daniel aside and let Paige and her animals pass. He kept a tight grip on Daniel while watching Paige. He couldn't shake the feeling the danger wasn't over. Maybe he was wary of the other shoe dropping. He'd lost her suddenly before. He'd nearly lost her again today. Would he ever be convinced she was safe?

They'd reached Paige's truck, parked on the side of the road at the head of the trail, before he breathed easier. Unclipping the keys from Daniel's belt loop, he unlocked the truck and shoved Daniel into the back seat. "Maverick and I will ride with him. You get the animals settled and drive."

"Sounds good." Paige lowered the tailgate and the rescues leaped into the back. "I'll tie them off so they don't—"

A figure wearing a red ski mask rushed from the underbrush near the truck, a raised knife glinting in the sun.

Paige screamed and ducked as the person swung the knife toward her. She dropped the leads and disappeared beneath the tailgate. The figure followed. Another shriek and the sounds of a fight followed.

"Paige!" Reece slammed the door to the truck and drew his weapon, racing for the rear of the vehicle.

There was a shriek and the masked figure rolled away from the truck, gripping one arm and running for the woods. Blood seeped through the clasping fingers.

"Paige!" Reece called her again, sliding to a stop as she rose, her shoulders heaving as she breathed heavily.

With a trembling hand, she held out the knife, blood on the blade.

Was she cut? Reece gingerly removed the weapon from her hand and laid it on the tailgate, scanning her from head to toe. Other than the tremors, she seemed to be safe.

She heaved in a deep breath. "I think I drew blood."

Blood was Maverick's wheelhouse. Calling his partner closer, he pointed to a drop of blood on the ground. While Mav wasn't a search dog or a bloodhound, he'd follow the trail to the end. "Search."

Nose to the ground, Maverick plunged into the woods.

Reece should follow him, but he also needed to protect Paige from the masked figure and from Daniel, who was still in the truck. He glanced into the wooded area Maverick had gone, where the sounds of crashing in the underbrush indicated his direction.

Holding out his gun grip-first toward Paige, he forced her to look at him. "Don't hesitate to defend yourself."

She stared at the weapon. "Reece, I can't take—"

A shriek tore through the woods, followed by a volley of wild barks from Maverick.

The crashing in the underbrush grew louder and Maverick's barks grew closer.

Reece almost smiled. His partner might not attack on command, but the German shepherd was intimidating and he'd follow evidence relentlessly. If Paige's attacker was running, Maverick wouldn't back off from his assigned task of finding the source of blood.

A figure burst from the woods. Reece was at the ready, weapon trained. "Rocky Mountain K-9 Officer. Stop, lace your fingers behind your head and get on your knees."

The attacker stopped, turning from Reece to Maverick and back again. Slowly, the person obeyed.

Circling cautiously behind, Reece reached forward and pulled away the mask.

Blond hair spilled out.

Callie Wyatt. Austin Wyatt's wife.

The rocky soil was damp beneath her, but Paige was past caring. Sitting in the enclosure with Camelot, she turned her face to the sun and wished it would burn away the morning's memories.

Daniel's frantic expression as he'd aimed the pistol, prepared to pull the trigger.

Callie Wyatt's murderous glare as she'd knelt on the ground, bleeding and defiant.

Austin Wyatt's grief-stained glower as he'd

exited the sheriff's office, trying to hold his head high in the aftermath of his wife's treachery.

Stomach swirling, Paige pressed her leg tighter against Camelot's back, drawing strength from the still-healing animal as he relaxed in the sun.

Near the driveway, Seb spoke in low tones into his cell phone, having received a call almost as soon as Camelot was safely back in his enclosure.

Paige had dropped beside the animal, needing to feel his unconditional love. It was hard to imagine Daniel having an affair with Callie. It was hard to imagine Callie using Wyatt to terrorize Paige so she could dangle the property as a peace offering if Austin ever discovered her infidelity.

It hurt Paige's brain to trace that line of thinking.

Austin's pain had been palpable as he'd left Sheriff Granger's office, blowing through the lobby where Paige waited to give her statement. She'd wanted to reach out, but she had nothing to offer a man whose wife had hidden so much.

Too many people were hiding things.

She'd hidden Hailey from Reece. Since he'd taken Callie into custody, they hadn't had a chance to speak. He was at the sheriff's department, working out logistics with federal authorities. Seb had picked her up and brought Camelot home as well. Now, she waited for Reece to return.

Maybe he wouldn't.

The thought brought pain to her already battered body. With the truth aired, her heart had taken license to draw toward him.

To love him.

Yet there was nothing she could do. No matter how understanding he'd acted before, he was bound to be more rational now, less willing to forgive so easily.

There was still the open issue of the land Noah had hidden from her. She wasn't sure she was ready to discover the reasons why.

"You okay?" Seb crouched beside her and reached to scratch Camelot's shoulder.

"Thinking." She stared at Seb's profile as he ran a practiced hand over Camelot's back. He'd been Noah's friend long before Paige had come along. "Did you have any idea Noah owned the land next to the refuge?"

"I did." Seb's chin dipped. "He talked to me about it once, probably a decade ago. It was something he was never comfortable with."

Paige's eyebrows pulled together. How could owning land be uncomfortable?

Jaw working back and forth, Seb seemed to chew his words. "Noah's great-grandfather won the land beside where the refuge sits in a bet with Brody Carson's great-grandfather. Problem is, family legend says he cheated."

Paige's eyes slipped shut. *Oh, Noah.* He'd been honest to a fault. "Even the hint of cheating would have disgusted him."

"It did." Seb nodded. "That land was an albatross. Selling it felt dishonest to him, but handing it to Brody for nothing when the refuge was constantly struggling didn't feel right either. When we talked, he said he was considering selling it to Brody for half its value. So when Brody started talking about the rafting center, I honestly thought he had."

"Why wouldn't he tell me?"

"I don't know."

Likely, he'd wrestled until the end, trying to find a way that was fair to the Carsons and to his own family.

Well, now she'd make things right. Seb's story confirmed her decision. "I'm selling Howling Moon." It was the only way, and the certainty of the plan brought a peace she hadn't felt in months. "I'll turn the other piece of land back over to Brody's family."

"I see." Nodding slowly, Seb sank back to sit

beside her. "Lacey and I have wondered for a while if you would."

"Really?"

"Yeah. It was a lot of work even when Noah was alive. With your donors vanishing and the town getting angrier every day… Paige, it's too much for one person. We'll find places for the animals, make sure they stay with their companions." That was Seb, always planning. "Austin may still want to buy the land you don't hand over to Brody. It would give you a good start."

"It would."

"There's that huge refuge near Denver we've traded animals with before. They've always liked you and your credentials. They might take some of these guys as well."

She'd already sent an email from her phone while they were waiting at the sheriff's office. The director had already texted her with a request to talk further.

If that went as she hoped, Hailey could be near her father.

With a doggie groan, Camelot eased to his feet and turned toward the driveway as the other rescues ran for the fences. A few seconds later, the sound of an engine drifted through the trees.

Paige didn't have to look. Her pulse picked up its pace at the sound of Reece's SUV.

"I'm going to get Hailey and Luna. We can talk when I get back." Seb rested his hand on her shoulder and stood. "Lacey and I will support you whatever you decide."

He was gone before she could answer. If she did leave Crystal Ridge behind, the hardest part would be saying goodbye to Seb and Lacey. Could she do it? Uproot everything for...

For her daughter to know her father.

Yes, she could.

Rising, she brushed dirt from her jeans and faced whatever Reece brought with him. Anger, acceptance...

Oh, let it be option two. Because if she'd discovered anything during this nightmare, it was that she loved Reece.

Paige rested her hands on her hips and watched Reece let Maverick out of the SUV. As he passed Seb, the two men paused briefly, spoke, then slapped each other on the back as they walked on.

Seb slammed the door on the Blazer and left.

Opening the gate, Reece strode into the enclosure, his eyes never breaking away from hers. There was an intention in his demeanor, one she heartily agreed with.

One that made her heart beat faster and her knees go wobbly.

When he was about six feet away, he stopped. Shoving his hands into his pockets, he simply… froze. His gaze slid away and back again, hesitant in a way she'd never seen before. For the first time, she caught a glimpse of what Reece might have been like as a little boy learning his place in the world. By the time she'd met him in high school, he'd seemed so self-assured.

Now, he'd slipped.

Because of her.

A weight rested against her calf and she glanced down. Camelot had approached and was leaning into her in the same way Luna often did. Whether it was to offer comfort or protection, she wasn't sure.

When the rescue looked up at her, it sure did bolster her courage.

Six years ago, she'd been afraid to speak up. Even three days ago, that fear had gripped her.

Now? Now she knew silence led nowhere. Truth would always be greater than any lie.

Thanks to Noah and the God he'd introduced her to, she also knew she was worthy of being loved and cherished.

So was Reece. Six years ago, she had fled without fully considering the damage she'd do to him, had been selfish with her love. Now she knew better.

She closed the gap between them and gently took his wrists, pulling his hands from his pockets then sliding her fingers down to clasp his.

It was the most terrifying thing she'd ever done. He could pull away. Reject her. He could—

The thought slammed to a halt when his lips found hers. His touch was familiar yet new. Comforting yet exhilarating.

She slipped her hands from his and slid her arms around his waist as he pulled her closer. Always protecting. Always sheltering.

Welcoming her and her healed heart into more than his embrace. He welcomed her into his life. Into his own healing heart.

Breaking the kiss, she rested her forehead against his shoulder and felt herself relax for the first time in… There was no way to calculate how long.

Reece tilted his head so his cheek rested against her hair. "We should talk."

Those words used to rock her with the fear she'd done something wrong. But now? In this cocoon between them, those words held the promise of next steps and future plans.

She couldn't wait to start. "I'm selling the refuge."

"I see." His voice rumbled low in his chest.

No longer hesitant. No longer questioning. "There's a hybrid sanctuary near Denver."

She smiled. "Seems I've had this conversation once already today."

"You have?" There was a gentle humor in his voice as he shifted her slightly and rested his forehead against hers.

"Yes. I've already reached out to them. They're interested."

"You'll need a place to live."

Oh, he was killing her with that low voice saying more between the lines than he was saying out loud. Her inhale was shaky with emotion. "I was thinking of buying a house with some acreage. Maybe a farm. A big place for a couple of the rescues to run. For Hailey to play. For her dad to get to know her."

"Her dad." His voice broke. Swallowing hard, he cleared his throat and tried again. "Maybe her mama and I should put together something permanent at that little farm you're talking about."

"Yeah?"

"I mean, after a nice long engagement where they get to know each other again." He pulled her gently closer. "I do have a ring already. In my closet in Denver. If you'd like to have it."

Her head dipped lower. This time, tears pricked. *He kept the ring.* For whatever reason, he'd kept the ring. She took a second to steady herself as her muscles all threatened to melt. She wanted to be certain her voice wouldn't shatter on emotion when she responded. "I would."

"Then we have a plan." He nuzzled her cheek with his chin, urging her to lift her chin. They met in another kiss, one that promised a new thing. A new love. A new future...where they'd rescue each other.

* * * * *

Don't miss Harlow Zane's story,
Tracking a Killer, *and the rest of the*
Rocky Mountain K-9 Unit series:

Dear Reader,

I wish you could see behind the scenes of the Rocky Mountain K-9 series! We have all had so much fun discussing the stories and the characters…and the puppers! I've loved working with all of these amazing authors, and we all hope you fall in love with these awesome dogs—and their people—as well!

While I was writing this book, my family lost both of our dogs to illnesses. Our sweet Dutch had been with us for thirteen years and was my best buddy to the end. Daisy was with us for nine years and was the sweetest girl you ever met. So, as I wrote this book, I was thinking a lot about the unconditional love our pets show us and how we are blessed to love them in return.

All of our pups have been rescues, and we got to bring them home and love them for their whole lives. In fact, just yesterday, we adopted a precious yellow Lab named Hattie. Her story would break your heart, but she's home now, and we get the privilege of loving her "furever."

Isn't it awesome that God rescues us too? That He brings us back home to Him through the sacrifice of Jesus? He cleans us up from our sins and He loves us with a love that can never be broken or taken away. Like the hybrid wolves at Paige's rescue center, people might misunderstand us or judge us, but God sees us for who we really are through the eyes of His love. That is a joy I can't express. To be a child of God… Have you ever stopped to think how amazing that is?

I hope you enjoy the Rocky Mountain K-9 series. I'd love to hear from you! You can drop by jodiebailey.com to find links to email and social media. And now, I'm off to shower our new pup with all of the pets that she can handle!

Jodie Bailey.

COUNTRY LEGACY COLLECTION

19 FREE BOOKS IN ALL!

Cowboys, adventure and romance await you in this new collection! Enjoy superb reading all year long with books by bestselling authors like Diana Palmer, Sasha Summers and Marie Ferrarella!

YES! Please send me the **Country Legacy Collection!** This collection begins with 3 FREE books and 2 FREE gifts in the first shipment. Along with my 3 free books, I'll also get 3 more books from the **Country Legacy Collection**, which I may either return and owe nothing or keep for the low price of $24.60 U.S./$28.12 CDN each plus $2.99 U.S./$7.49 CDN for shipping and handling per shipment*. If I decide to continue, about once a month for 8 months, I will get 6 or 7 more books but will only pay for 4. That means 2 or 3 books in every shipment will be FREE! If I decide to keep the entire collection, I'll have paid for only 32 books because 19 are FREE! I understand that accepting the 3 free books and gifts places me under no obligation to buy anything. I can always return a shipment and cancel at any time. My free books and gifts are mine to keep no matter what I decide.

☐ 275 HCK 1939   ☐ 475 HCK 1939

Name (please print)

Address   Apt. #

City   State/Province   Zip/Postal Code

Mail to the Harlequin Reader Service:
IN U.S.A.: P.O. Box 1341, Buffalo, NY 14240-8571
IN CANADA: P.O. Box 603, Fort Erie, Ontario L2A 5X3

*Terms and prices subject to change without notice. Prices do not include sales taxes, which will be charged (if applicable) based on your state or country of residence. Canadian residents will be charged applicable taxes. Offer not valid in Quebec. All orders subject to approval. Credit or debit balances in a customer's account(s) may be offset by any other outstanding balance owed by or to the customer. Please allow 3 to 4 weeks for delivery. Offer available while quantities last. © 2021 Harlequin Enterprises ULC. ® and ™ are trademarks owned by Harlequin Enterprises ULC.

Your Privacy—Your information is being collected by Harlequin Enterprises ULC, operating as Harlequin Reader Service. To see how we collect and use this information visit https://corporate.harlequin.com/privacy-notice. From time to time we may also exchange your personal information with reputable third parties. If you wish to opt out of this sharing of your personal information, please visit www.readerservice.com/consumerchoice or call 1-800-873-8635. Notice to California Residents—Under California law, you have specific rights to control and access your data. For more information visit https://corporate.harlequin.com/california-privacy.

50BOOKCL22